The GIPSY *in the* PARLOUR

The GIPSY
in the
PARLOUR

by
MARGERY SHARP

Little, Brown and Company · Boston

TO
GEOFFREY CASTLE

PART ONE

CHAPTER I

I

In the heat of a spacious August noon, in the heart of the great summer of 1870, the three famous Sylvester women waited in their parlour to receive and make welcome the fourth.

Themselves matched the day. The parlour was hot as a hothouse, not a window was open, all three women were big, strongly-corsetted, amply-petticoated, layered chin to toe in flannel, cambric, and silk at a guinea a yard. Their broad, handsome faces were scarlet, their temples moist. But they stood up to the heat of the parlour as they stood up to the heat of the kitchen or the heat of a harvest-field: as the sun poured in upon them so their own strong good-humour flowed out to meet it—to refract and multiply it, like the prisms of their candlesticks, the brass about their hearth. Nature had so cheerfully designed them that even wash-day left them fair-tempered: before the high festivity of a marriage their spirits rose, expanded, and bloomed to a solar pitch of stately jollification.

Everything in the parlour shone. After the prisms and the andirons the two most striking points of brillance were a china-cabinet, its panes so diamond-like that light must merely have bounced back, but for the attraction of the lustre-ware within, and the gilding of a tall, scroll-worked harp. The floor reflected

3

the furniture: a pair of water-clear mirrors reflected each other. The grandfather-clock was a column of amber. (A smaller, dimmer sun ornamenting its face.) At the windows, long curtains, of very old brocade, showed their original bright crimson at each turn of a fold: a square of Turkey carpet, equally ancient, equally proclaimed the excellence of old dyes.—It was a room, in short, worth the sun's while to shine on; and that it was so, and that it was also the heart of the great sprawling house, half-manor and half-farm, was the Sylvester women's triumph.

They had won no easy victory. The men they wedded were masterful as themselves: black as they were golden, strong-willed and strong-backed: apt to eat in the kitchen, and without (till the first bride came home) sluicing themselves. This original Amazon was my Aunt Charlotte, wife of the eldest son Tobias; her two sisters-in-law were of her own choosing—equally high-coloured, equally high-handed, equally apt to civilize the black Sylvester males. The fourth Sylvester woman, the awaited betrothed, my youngest Uncle Stephen chose for himself; and until that morning only he had set eyes on her.

2

ONE must go back. I go back—how willingly!—to the night some four years earlier when I first arrived, a small sickly girl-child, in my Aunt Charlotte's kitchen. My parents were Londoners: I had coughed all a smoky winter, a chill spring: with the summer I was sent down to these half-known connections to try the benefit of West Country air. I was then

4

seven years old, and obviously did not travel alone; I remember
adult (though unfamiliar) company in the train; but towards
the end of the journey some arrangement must have broken
down, for I made its last stage, by carrier's cart, in charge solely
of the carrier, and when I arrived it was quite dark. My Aunt
Charlotte unwrapped me from my shawls, set me up on the
great kitchen table, and with a loud cry of distress instantly
gave me a honey-comb. I hadn't a spoon, I couldn't, for cold and
weariness, have eaten if I had; but the impetuous welcoming
gesture—I still see the upward sweep of a great creamy arm—
gave me an extraordinary sensation of happiness.

I felt, for my mind then fed on fairy-tales, like the girl in the
story whom an enormous kindly cat popped into a jug of magic
milk, which turned her golden.

This image quite remarkably persisted. To me, a cockney of
cockneys, living at the farm was like living amongst great kindly
creatures not quite of my own race. Every object, from the
huge horses in the stables to the huge cream-pans in the dairy,
was so astoundingly large. My four uncles and their sire moved
particularly enormous. I didn't see much of them, I was kept
mewed like a parlour-boarder from all mucky farm-activity; but
my Aunt Charlotte loomed almost as gigantic. To me she was
tall as a sunflower—and like a sunflower wore a great golden
crown, that unplaited fell to her knees. Her hands were man-
size and brown, but her arms and shoulders milk-white; her
eyes, like her mouth, smiled easily, but her lightest love-tap—
I was often underfoot—sent me half across the kitchen. It was
easy to comprehend how she had made the first breach in the
bachelorhood of the Sylvester men.

The tale was legendary, and deserved to be: until her coming

the old widower and his four sons having lived like so many
Orsons or savages, with for all female influence one old witch
in the kitchen. Yet they owned their land and wheat stood at
over forty shillings: old Mr. Sylvester could have been church-
warden—save that he never went to church. (They none of
them went to church.) Their dwelling-house, originally a
manor, was not only commodious, but handsome. (Or might
have been, had they spent the least pains on it; which they
never did.) The older portion was so picturesque that summer-
visitors came to sketch it: there are contemporary water-colours
without number, of the broad, sodded court lying between the
manor's two wings.

It was formerly infested, this court, by donkeys. When old
Mr. Sylvester bought all and for a peppercorn, he was forced
to turn out a great number of gipsies who through the winter
roosted there: so much had the estate decayed, by death, extravagance and misfortune. The greensward was invaded by
thistles, upon which natural pasture fed the gipsies' donkeys,
the space bounded by the two crumbling wings and the main
bulk of the house forming a sort of corral for them. Old Mr.
Sylvester rigorously turned both gipsies and donkeys out, and
moved in with his growing four sons. They were Tobias, Matthew, Luke and Stephen; who with their sire took root and
flourished.

They were savages, but they didn't neglect the land. Where
land was concerned they were even progressive. They brought
in the first mechanical thresher their neighbours had ever seen.
They sent to Plymouth for guano, buying it straight from the
ship. As farmers, and as a team of five strong men, they waxed,
for farmers, rich. Old Mr. Sylvester could have been a Justice

—save that he wasn't able, or pretended not to be able, to spell his name.

His four sons remained bachelors, but notoriously assuaged, after market-day, and in the lowest quarters, their natural masculine powers. Fortunately they weren't quarrelsome, and had heads like rocks, for they drank enough for eight. Whatever they did there was no one to check them, no one to say them nay—until Tobias the eldest, foraying into Norfolk after a ram, was himself brought to market by my Aunt Charlotte.

She was quite simply the finest woman he'd ever seen. She stood five-foot-nine in her stockings, and her head was Ceres'—gold-braided, high-coloured, smiling abundance. My Aunt Charlotte saw a black, six-footer eldest son. Her father owned the ram Tobias had his eye on; she, looking queen-like over the best Norfolk could offer, signalled her acceptance of an alliance which Tobias willingly allowed himself to have proposed. He had to wait in Norfolk four weeks longer, while the banns were called; and employed the interval to write a letter home.

Dear father, dear brothers (wrote Tobias),

I'm to be wed Tuesday two weeks. Wednesday two weeks expect me home. The young woman sends her respects, and I have got a ram.

I have said that my Aunt Charlotte's home-coming was legendary; like a legend, it lost nothing in the re-telling. The first object that met her eyes, on her arrival at her new home, was a donkey in the kitchen. This was explicable, if at the time disconcerting; one or two strays of the race still remembered their old haunt in the courtyard, and the kitchen-door, which abutted it, swung on a broken hinge. Tobias should properly

7

have set down his bride at the great main door, but there was the ram, under a net, in the back of their cart: he drove straight round into the court, it was mizzling with rain, and Charlotte ran for the nearest shelter. The donkey and she met head-on: without the slightest hesitation she snatched up a broom, thwacked it across the quarters, and drove it out. Immediately over the threshold a morass of poached mud sucked at her new shoes. She turned back into the kitchen, spied a pair of pattens, put them on and returned to the attack. The braying of the beast she so harried rose like a gipsy's warning: still my Aunt Charlotte thwacked. When Tobias returned from the byre he found his bride, in pattens, already beating the bounds of her new demesne.

3

"DEAR souls, but I was wrathful!" related my Aunt Charlotte. "So wrathful was I, I'd hardly let 'un bed me!"

And it was indeed the fact that she not only unpacked her own sheets, and her own goose-feather pillows, but also gave the nuptial chamber a good turn-out, before her groom was allowed upstairs. Raging all the while—but she raged as the sun shone, from inexhaustible reserves of heat and power—my Aunt Charlotte drove the cross old serving-woman before her to sweep, thump, sluice and air, while in the kitchen below the four celibate Sylvesters sat in grimly humorous surveillance of the groom. They had cider enough to sustain them, but— "Don't you make 'un drunk, bors!" shouted the bride, down the stairs, from time to time. It was two in the morning before

Tobias was admitted; but then, such was Charlotte's super-abundant vitality, enjoyed a thoroughly successful bedding.

At precisely seven o'clock next morning, she served porridge, pork, eggs and hollow biscuits to all who had previously soused their heads under the pump. No sousing, no breakfast. All soused.

Thus the Sylvester men knew at once what they were in for. So did my Aunt Charlotte. The household she entered was as roughly bounteous, and almost as uncivilized, as a camp of successful robbers. She had five men to tame as she might have had five hawks. Half the rooms of her house were shut or mildewed, and her courtyard was infested with donkeys. But she had certain advantages. Like all primitive people, the Sylvesters admired first physical strength, then physical beauty: before the combination of both, and in such measure, as displayed by Tobias' wife, they were from the first ready to treat. Not to surrender: Charlotte never had it all her own way. She never, for example, got her father-in-law into a clean neckerchief, save on Sundays. She never got the dogs—though she got the donkeys—out of her court. Life at the farm became for years one long, pitched, enjoyable battle, in which each side found a certain satisfaction in the other's victories. My Aunt Charlotte was proud of her five wild men; so were the five wild men proud of my Aunt Charlotte's parlour.

It didn't immediately, of course, reach its later pitch of perfection. It had been so long disused that there was difficulty even in finding the key, and the sight that met Charlotte's eyes, when first the door groaned open, would have daunted Hercules. On the floor dust lay thicker than the carpet, at the windows hung cobwebs more substantial than the curtains: the

harp careened like an unrigged ghostly skiff, and at some point
a nestful of rooks must have fallen down the chimney, before
which their mummified bodies still lay.

But the curtains were brocade. They went to Charlotte's
head. In a matter of days she had rummaged through enough
old account-books—unhandled by any Sylvester male—to pronounce them woven at Lyons, France. They had cost, those
curtains, in the year 1760, no less than fifty pounds; and if this
was but another proof of the extravagance that ruined their
original owners, Charlotte saw no reason why she shouldn't
profit by it. An ancient woman, skilled in the use of soapwort,
was summoned to soak and cleanse them: the repairing, almost
the re-weaving of them, went on for years. Meanwhile Charlotte
polished at the floor, and at the marble of a high carved chim-
neypiece. From Norfolk there presently arrived furniture of
some state—a mahogany gate-leg table, the glass-fronted china-
cabinet, a wing-chair covered with needlework—to be set about
the Turkey carpet; and if the whole was immediately declared
forbidden ground to all in muddy boots, it says much for Charlotte's large-mindedness that she let any one in at all. Parlours
less fine by half, in that community, were never entered from
Christmas to Christmas. But Charlotte not only allowed her
parlour to be used, she insisted on it—every Sunday. Every
Sunday evening her five wild men had to clean up and present
themselves for an hour of genteel slumber. Old Mr. Sylvester
slept in the wing-chair. He actually preferred the familiar
spokes of a wheel-back, but Charlotte decreed the other more
fitting. She herself wasn't particularly comfortable on the
piano-stool, but she felt it fitting that she should sit on *it*, after
achieving such a crowning parlour-glory as a piano . . .

I wish I had known the house in those stirring, embattled days. When I came to it it was complete, ripe in its golden prime. Every room was open, and furnished, and aired; there was even a flower-bed—the farmer's last luxury—ablow under the parlour windows. I took it all for granted. That I was the first to *play* on the parlour piano meant at the time nothing to me; and if I still recall, as I tinkled out 'Bluebells of Scotland', the enraptured faces of my three aunts, I re-savour chiefly my own conceit. I didn't realise that I was setting the gilded crown on an edifice twenty years a-building.—Indeed, that perhaps came later, when I taught all my aunts 'Chopsticks', and we used to play it four-handed. . . .

What *I* longed for was to play upon the harp. It was an instrument already so out-of-date as to have become romantic. But there was no one to teach me, and I doubt if I should have made an apt pupil. I did sometimes, plucking at an unbroken string, draw forth a single melancholy twang; but no one played on the harp, it was never put in order, not even when my Uncle Stephen brought home his Welsh bride.

4

THE brides of my Uncles Matthew and Luke (who are still waiting in the parlour), were brought home by Charlotte.

Her motive was at once practical and altruistic. She had more on her hands than any one female could manage, and she also thought it shame to leave any able-bodied male unbadgered into matrimony. "What's us women to do, if 'ee toads won't wed us?" demanded my Aunt Charlotte vigorously—but without ever receiving a satisfactory answer. The Sylvester men had simply settled down under her energetic and beneficent sway: openly enjoying their increased comforts, calling Tobias to his face a lucky hero, but showing not the least disposition to follow his example. Great handsome chaps as they were, too! "What's the matter with 'ee?" railed my Aunt Charlotte. "What's lacking, that 'ee don't bring me home some women?" The old man said nothing; the three bachelors grinned. Charlotte knew as well as they where they went after market, though convention forbade her admitting it. What was the matter with them was that they were bone-selfish, they didn't want to be bothered with the ritual of proper courting. It was less demanding to take what they needed, pay for it fair and square, and let Tobias do respectable for all. . . .

Charlotte therefore took matters into her own hands, looked about as she'd have looked about for a dairy-maid—though naturally with stricter requirements—and pitched on my Aunt Grace.

Her nature was essentially big. She was big all round, big in her high-coloured handsomeness, her untiring energy, her unfailing good-humour. Other women in her position might have looked for sisters-in-law creep-mouse, docile, unpretending. Not so my Aunt Charlotte. She already saw herself thoroughly a Sylvester, matriarch of a tribe that had all big and handsome about them. So she pitched on Grace Beer, daughter of a farmer the other side of Frampton—strapping almost as herself, even blonder as to high-piled coiffure, and equally famous with poultry. The two women had been on visiting-terms for some months: Miss Beer, unlike Charlotte, (here we refer to one of my Aunt Charlotte's defeats), commanded her own pony-trap, in which she spanked through the lanes like a female Phaeton. As a rule she appeared only at an hour when the men were afield; around four in the afternoon, for instance, when Charlotte elegantly refreshed her with gooseberry-wine. On a certain Sunday, however, she arrived, obviously by pre-arrangement, to partake of a particularly recherché supper, and afterwards to sit in the parlour, genteelly conversing with her friend before the conscript audience of Sylvester men. As soon as she left, Charlotte delivered an ultimatum.

"Well, there she is, bors," said my Aunt Charlotte. "Her father'll give her a hundred pounds, and I've seen her linen myself. Which is it to be, Matthew or Luke?"

After a short but pregnant pause, Matthew enquired, Why not Stephen?

"Because she doesn't fancy a youngest. She'll take you or Luke—and I tell 'ee all now, I mean to have another female along wi' me before my time."

She was expecting her first child in two months. She must have looked, as she faced her menfolk, a very Ceres, a very Venus Genetrix indeed. They knew she hadn't so far ailed a day; they also recognized the validity of her claim. Not a word was said, but all eyes turned on Matthew; seniority has duties as well as rights. To do him justice, he went through his court-ing like a man. The next three Sundays in succession saw him driving doggedly over beyond Frampton in best coat, clean shirt, brushed hat; he heard the banns called without flinching, and in due course was got to church on time. The Sylvester defences thus doubly breached, my Uncle Luke, when Char-lotte a year later produced my future Aunt Rachel, went to the slaughter like a lamb.

Rachel's chief (and complementary) talent was for dairy-work. She also was exceedingly handsome, built on the same lavish scale as her sisters-in-law, fair, kind, and gentle in her ways; so my Uncle Luke had no bad bargain.

I am told that for the next few years one couldn't set foot in the farm without treading an infant. They were all—as though the tamed Sylvester men in this reasserted themselves —males. Loudly as my aunts complained, religiously as they followed every local rite of girl-producing birth-magic, boy after boy swarmed from his cradle. (At one time there were no less than three a-rock together: in due course no fewer than seven urchins made a bedlam of the farmyard.) I think now this was partly the reason why I myself was made so welcome. I should have been made welcome in any case, from sheer goodness of heart, because I looked so small and sickly; but I was also a girl-child, such as those three fecund women had never been able to produce. . . . Moreover, by the time I appeared not even a son was left to them; it being a characteristic of the Sylvester male that he needed plenty of room. The farm couldn't hold them, and their Dads—no Sylvester minced words —seeming so solid as rocks, the young ones scattered—as far off as Canada and Australia, there to set up, on opposite sides of the globe, new robber-households of their own. Thus I was doubly welcome; and though I was ever the young lady, the bird of passage, my aunts loved me as a last child of the house. What their love meant to me is something I cannot yet assess.

I had never before encountered love. In London, at home, I was being well brought up, and well educated; but I wasn't being loved. Ours was a cold household, in London; though my mother loved both my brothers, so well that in due course both their wives left them. My father I think loved no one. What I found at the farm was something so new, so excellent, that my summers there now appear to me like summers in a golden age. Yet how would I have described, at the time, that honey-gold warmth of love?—I should have said merely that my aunts were very kind to me, and got on together very well.

That of course is the clue. They got on together, the three big women, so famously. They liked each other. All through the day their loud cheerful talk ran in one long triple conversation, shouted, if necessary, between room and room, so that no one missed anything. Charlotte always and naturally held rather the upper hand. She was the *first* of the Sylvester women. It was she who drove out the donkeys. Proper marriage-feasts, proper marriage-chambers, welcomed first Grace, then Rachel: if they didn't realise, she soon enough told them what barbarity they'd been spared. But she never played the despot; it was essentially as equals that they presented a solid front to their five wild men, it was essentially as equals that they now enjoyed such pride in their house and their husbands and their parlour.—Rachel contributed the lustre-ware: Grace, the furniture for the hearth. When they'd burnished the place for Sunday they used to stand so proud as three peacocks. And when, once a month, they'd stood prouder still, nudging their three big husbands into the Sylvester *pew*—"Only us could have tamed 'em!" triumphed my Aunt Charlotte. "Us three Sylvester women!"

SHE didn't bother to marry Stephen. There seemed no point in it. Stephen was left in peace, at thirty-five still the solitary bachelor, the perpetual youngest brother—and my favourite uncle.

This was inevitable, since none of the others took the least notice of me. I think they regarded me much as they would have regarded a pet lamb, brought in by the women and to be brought up by them. I regarded *them* with awe: to me they were like forces of nature—huge, silent, unarguable. Certainly I shouldn't have described them as particularly tame; on the other hand, they had stopped being wild as hawks. (Their father, eighty-odd, was like a little old falcon: white with age, blinking on his perch by the fire.) They had come to partake, under their wives' influence and with their own maturity, more of the nature of tors, or rocks. I suppose my Uncle Tobias, when I first knew him, wasn't much over fifty; to me he was old as the hills. My Uncle Stephen, on the other hand, partly because he wasn't married, partly because he hadn't a beard, I regarded almost as a contemporary. But undoubtedly I loved him best for the one simple reason, that he noticed me.

He used sometimes to set me to ride home on a haywain. He quite often used to take me to see birds'-nests. Once he even took me fishing—when I disgraced myself by falling in, and he plunged after, and we returned in equal disgrace to the scoldings of Aunt Charlotte. She instantly flung me into a boiling-hot bath before the kitchen-fire, then hurled me into bed with a cup of black-currant tea. I do not imagine she personally soused my Uncle Stephen also, but when I asked him, next day, whether he'd been made to drink the tea, he admitted that he had.

As he was the youngest of the brothers, so he was the smallest: by Sylvester standards, small absolutely. His black thatch of hair came to Tobias' shoulder, Matthew's chin, Luke's ear; that they were all exceptionally tall, giants even in a countryside of giants, did not make Stephen's lack of stature, among his kindred, any less noticeable. He was the lightweight Sylvester—lanky as his brothers were ponderous, sallow rather than swarthy, narrower as to skull and cheekbone, less voluntary as to mouth and eye. I secretly considered his appearance interesting; my aunts openly lamented he'd never got his full growth. They loved him and laughed at him and spoiled him; and when he at last, all on his own, found himself a wife, thought it the greatest joke in the world.

They were no more jealous or disturbed than three big suns. When the letter came from Plymouth, whither Stephen had been sent after guano, my aunts laughed all morning. However'd he managed it, they demanded, with no woman to push him forward? "The cunning toad!" cried my Aunt Charlotte, wiping tears of laughter from her eyes. "If he b'aint the boldest Sylvester yet!"

The preparations went forward on a gale of hilarity. My aunts cooked every viand they could lay hands on, turned out the parlour, changed round all the furniture in a bedroom, and with half an hour to spare stood waiting as I have described them—hot, gorgeous and jocund—to welcome Stephen's bride.

It is 1870; I am eleven years old.

CHAPTER II

I

HE entered first; then she, stepping close behind him: small, very slender, rather limply dressed in black or grey, on her head a small black straw hat. There was an air of the town about her; and of something else which I, (staring out from behind my aunts), couldn't immediately define. For an instant no one moved: the air was suddenly heavy, as though all the great house, all the broad fields beyond, pressed in upon us with a shared expectancy. From under the brim of her hat Miss Davis' swift, bright glance flickered once over the room, then dropped; my Uncle Stephen's hand never left her shoulder.—The next moment the spell was broken, my Aunt Charlotte had swooped forward—kissed the bride, kissed Stephen, passed them back to be re-kissed by Grace and Rachel, dragged me up too—but I kissed only Stephen—and the right uproar of welcome exploded like a feu de joie. I have said the parlour was like a hot-house. I was so hot myself, in my best alpaca, that I came close to being sick. I couldn't distinguish a word that was said, it was all one loud babel of greeting, questions, congratulation. Then Miss Davis was bustled away, my Uncle Stephen went to seek his brothers, and I was left alone.

I didn't know what to do with myself. So I sat down at the piano and played 'Chopsticks.'

2

It was by now a characteristic of the Sylvester men that one could never tell what they were thinking. Such thoughts as they wished, or needed, to communicate, they put into words, otherwise they effortlessly preserved complete inscrutability. This trait was peculiarly apparent that night at supper, which was the first occasion of their meeting with Stephen's betrothed; they naturally hadn't come in, from harvesting, to see someone they would see daily for the rest of their lives. My Uncle Stephen presented her with due formality; in due order, starting with old Mr. Sylvester, the Sylvester men pronounced exactly as many words as were necessary for her due salutation; but whether Stephen's choice was any more than accepted —whether it was approved, or not approved—remained unknown. A Sylvester male was always rather silent at table, the better the fare, the less he spoke; and since my aunts had spread what was practically a marriage-feast, any apparent glumness meant nothing. But Stephen too relapsed into his home-manners, and the talk was left all to the women.

My three aunts talked splendidly.

I choose the word with intent. As a rule their continual loud conversation flowed in a spate of broad Devonian, varied by an occasional touch of Norfolk from Charlotte; but they had all received quite grand educations in their time, my Aunt Grace had even been to boarding-school, and when they chose they could out-niminy any lady in the shire. They did so now. With elegance and adjectives, with pronouns and prepositions each in the right place, they discoursed fashion, society and the arts. My Aunt Rachel had once witnessed, in Exeter, a performance of Hamlet; my Aunt Charlotte, in youth, had taken drawing-lessons with a pupil of Mr. Crome of Norwich; while my Aunt Grace shone particularly in the account of a charity-bazaar opened by the Duchess of Somerset.

I listened with awe. I peered eagerly at Miss Davis to see her bowled over. (Her first name was Myfanwy, which in Stephen's letter my aunts had hardly been able to make out; so they called her Fanny.) I couldn't see much of her, for she was placed directly the other side of my Uncle Matthew, it was like peering round a rock at a wren; but she seemed to be sitting quite composedly, attentive, but not dumbfounded . . . When she spoke it was always to agree: she too admired the works of Shakespeare; she too admired the landscapes of Mr. Crome; and if she had never seen the Duchess of Somerset, longed above all things to do so. . . .

She had a peculiarly sweet voice. I noticed it at once. It was low, small, (as one calls a singing-voice small), made musical by a faint Welsh lilt. It was a *wooing* voice. Yet when she spoke to *me*—peering in her turn round my Uncle Matthew to ask how old I was—I answered rather surlily. The voices I was used to, at the farm, were the big carrying voices of my Aunts Grace and Rachel and Charlotte; I was used to being, however lovingly, *bawled* at. This newcomer's sweetness struck me as something alien; and so I answered sulkily.

One naturally hadn't the least idea what the Sylvester men made of this cultured flow. If they were proud of their womenfolk they didn't show it, and if they were bored or bothered they didn't show that either. They simply and Homerically ate. I couldn't see my Uncle Stephen at all, he was on Miss Davis' farther side; whatever looks or words of affection they might have been exchanging, I couldn't see, or hear, either.

Immediately after the meal I was sent to bed. The consequences were as one would expect: I had consumed—my uncles, however otherwise oblivious of me, never neglected to heap my plate—enough rich and varied food to upset an alderman. I had wolfed raised-pie and custard-pie, spiced ham and cheese-cakes. I awoke, at what seemed to me long after midnight, still so oppressed by goblin-dreams that I slipped out of my bed and crept for reassurance to the never-failing succour of my Aunt Charlotte's strong hand.

(In the upbringing of children all that matters is love. My Aunt Charlotte encouraged me to over-eat, sent me over-early to bed, and when nightmares chased me out of it, smacked me. Each stage of this deplorable sequence was so informed by love that I never failed to return to peaceful sleep. Her big, offhand smack, like the cuff of an amiable lioness, carried more love with it than most kisses I have known since.)

As soon as I reached the landing, my mistake was apparent; even eleven hadn't struck. From below came the rumbling voices of my uncles—their tongues at last released from ceremony. I knew then that I had stumbled on the best time of all; the women had just come upstairs, I should find my Aunt Charlotte alone; she wouldn't have to lean out and just smack me cursorily, over my Uncle Tobias' huge bulk. She might even, after smacking me, let me stay and watch while she unplaited and brushed her hair. I padded on, already assuaged.

But of the two doors I had first to pass, one stood ajar; curiosity impelled me to pause, and ferret a step forward, and look in; and at once the new, sweet voice addressed me.

"Is that the little girl? Come in, dear."

I hesitated. But I had no reason to draw back, I was inquisitive, and my new aunt's voice was peculiarly alluring. (So soon I forgot that it was alien.) I went in. The room that had been given her wasn't small, none of the rooms were small, but it was comparatively bare; an enormous amount of space stretched in all directions round the shabby carpetbag half-emptied in the middle of the floor. Shyness made me fix my eyes on it: it had a pattern of big purplish roses, faded almost to the buff of the ground.

"Come closer, dear," said Fanny Davis.

I approached. The dressing-table before which she sat was candle-lit; by their double flames we contemplated each other through the mirror. Without her hat, without the net she had worn at supper, my new aunt looked much younger. Her short dark hair, which she was brushing, stood out in a smoky bush, very soft and fine, yet peculiarly alive—as though it would crackle under the brush as mine did sometimes in a thunder-storm. But it wasn't what I have been brought up to consider pretty hair. It couldn't compare with my Aunt Charlotte's. The face it haloed was small and pale; the eyes looking back at me through the glass, grey, with short dark lashes, were to me un-beautiful. Altogether I marvelled how my Uncle Stephen, used to the splendid Sylvester women, could have fallen in love with such a thin, pale, dusky little gipsy.

Miss Davis smiled, and from the littered dresser picked out a small paper bag.

"Do you like sweets, little girl?"

This put me in something of a quandary. I did like sweets, and though I couldn't have eaten one exactly then, might have saved it till morning; but all my real aunts set their faces against shop-made confectionery. (They said it was kept under the shop-keepers' beds. Now and again, when they had time, they made me toffee; or sometimes I was allowed to make it for myself, from sugar and our own butter.) The sweets in the proffered bag were fat satiny cushions, suspiciously striped, and moreover the bag itself was imperfectly clean. I felt quite certain that my Aunt Grace would immediately have put all behind the fire. I was also afraid of catching scarlet fever. (Scarlet fever germs notoriously pullulating beneath shop-keepers' beds.) However, I had been specially instructed to be polite; so I took one, with an appropriate mumble.

"If you're my little friend, you shall have sweets every day," promised Miss Davis. "Sit down, dear, on the bed, and talk to me."

I sat, but found I had nothing to say. I was quite glad when she began to ask me questions.

"I suppose *I* must be causing a great flutter here?" suggested she.

I thought this over. Children often understand, when an adult questions them, what meaning underlies the surface words. Recalling my aunts' enormous activities both above and below stairs, I nonetheless replied, No. I said everyone just seemed pleased.

"Which is the very sweetest thing I could have heard!" cried Miss Davis; but paused a moment, while she brushed her hair right and left into a new halo. I waited. "My dear Stephen

24

told me what I might expect," said Miss Davis, brushing away, "but really, three such beauties!" Gathering that she meant my aunts, I nodded. "Still, Mrs. Toby is by far the handsomest. I'm sure *that's* generally accepted?"

Translating Mrs. Toby into my Aunt Charlotte, I muttered that I liked her hair.

"Beside which *mine* is no more than a sweep's mop?" agreed Miss Davis—I thought very properly. Even when she fluffed it out, it wasn't thick. "And as *Mr.* Toby's the eldest, and *she's* his wife—I suppose she has things pretty much her own way?"

I didn't know what to answer. Of course my Aunt Charlotte had things her own way—in the house; but as *her* way was so identically that of my other aunts Grace and Rachel, the implication—which I sensed—was quite wrong. I picked my words.

"I don't think there's any difference," I explained. "I mean, all my aunts get their way, because it's the same. . . ."

My new Aunt Fanny regarded me, I thought, impatiently.

"The eldest is always the eldest," said she—and suddenly, with that little characteristic flicker, dropped her eyes. "And which of your *uncles* do you think the handsomest?" she asked.

I said, Stephen. I knew he wasn't really, but I wished to give her pleasure. I thought it was with pleasure that she laughed. —Just a little jet of laughter, higher-pitched than her usual tones.

"So we agree on all points," said Miss Davis. "I see you really *are* to be my little friend . . ."

I shifted uneasily on the bed. I was conscious that I ought really to be in my own. I was conscious that I hadn't, somehow, given the right answers to her questions. At the same time—

and how often, during our relationship, was that phrase, that alternative, to recur!—at the same time, I was fascinated. The semi-secrecy of the whole episode: the swift motion of Miss Davis' fingers as, still earnestly regarding me, she plaited up her hair; even the two big tortoiseshell combs with which at last she pinned it—all was unusual, and therefore fascinating. At last she fell silent, sitting to look, with a long scrutinizing gaze, at her own reflection; and I got up off the bed. She turned.

"And what do I get, for my bag of sweets?" she asked. "Don't I get a kiss?"

I wasn't sufficiently fascinated not to hesitate. She rose, and swiftly, soundlessly, like a moth, dipped towards me past the candles. Her kiss was pressing, and very soft. As I bundled myself from the room I heard her laugh.

I didn't pad on, that night, to my Aunt Charlotte's room beyond. I went back to my own.

3

WHAT I am now about to relate is what I physically saw.

My window overlooked a small grass-plot in which grew a crab-apple. That I have not mentioned this crab before must not be allowed to diminish its importance: in a way it was as much a triumph of my Aunt Charlotte's as was her parlour, for a pippin would have flourished there equally: the crab grubbed up, one might have planted a Cox's Orange. My Aunt Charlotte kept the crab, for no other reason than its prettiness.

It was the prettiest thing I had ever seen. (Or, for that matter, ever have seen.) Its slender trunk was most exquisitely

canopied by·a small pagoda of brilliant, rustling leaves: for its
fruits, delicately warming, with summer, from ivory to coral,
I never found a comparison until many years later I observed
the bill of a black swan. Charlotte, when they were ripe, could
have made jelly from them—which would have given the tree
some sort of economic standing; that she didn't was yet one
more proof of her remarkable character. She'd made Tobias
spare that tree, she once told me, for its prettiness alone, when
she came as a bride; she wouldn't climb down now and make
jelly.—I threw myself into eager support of such aestheticism,
and strove for hours, with a paper and a box of crayons, to im-
mortalise the beauty of our crab.

That night, (I return to *my* return to my own room), a
brilliant moonlight drew me irresistibly to the window. It had
been so hot all day that the wood of the window-seat was still
faintly warm; I tucked up my nightgown to kneel on bare
knees; the sill was warm under my elbows. Yet in the court
below—what ravishment!—the crab-tree appeared frosted, so
meticulously did the moon's white light rime every bough and
twig. It was a little tree done in silver-point; and so beautiful,
thus colourless, that I mentally renounced my chalks for ever.
I stared out, ravished—and as I gazed, saw the tree's cast shadow,
(where it lay most spreadingly, a stencilled pagoda), disengage
a shadow that moved.

Out of the shadow of the crab-tree stepped first the shadow,
then the figure, of Fanny Davis, whom I had just left seated
at her dressing-table.

She stood looking at the house. I saw her plainly. It was no
trick of moonlight; no moon-trick ever produced image so solid,
likeness so doppelgänger-exact. I saw her.

My panic, for it was panic, fixed itself on one point: that she might see me. I crouched down on the window-seat, flattening myself below the sill; thence at last to slide stiffly to the floor, and creep into my cold bed.

4

WITH morning, of course, everything became explicable. I saw that I had made an error in judging what time elapsed since I left Miss Davis' room. No doubt I ran straight from her door to the window-seat: but quite probably fell straight asleep on it. It could have been an hour later, or two hours, before I awoke to see Fanny Davis under the crab. (I was perfectly certain it was no dream.) As to *why* she was there, my romantic imagination easily supplied an answer: she had gone to meet my Uncle Stephen.—I have already described the milling jollity of their welcome; the one thing no one seemed to have imagined, for one instant, was that the lovers might wish some little time alone . . .

I was so pleased with my perspicacity, I ran out early to examine the ground under the little tree. I hoped to find footprints—hers narrow and pointed, my Uncle Stephen's horseshoe-broad. But there had been no rain for a week, the ground about the crab was like iron: Assemblies could have danced there, without leaving a trace.

CHAPTER III

I

THE wedding was set for a month off, just time, (so all Sylvesters wedded), to call the banns; the betwixt-and-between interval, while Fanny Davis hung poised between maiden- and matron-hood, was characterized, so to speak, by being *un*characterized.

It was a month just like any other. Nothing was changed. The torrent of my aunts' talk rushed loud and unceasing through the house with never a new note in it. Admittedly one had to be quick, one had to shout, to get a word in, and Miss Davis' voice was peculiarly soft; but in the early days at least my aunts used actually to *pause,* to check themselves and wait, to give her a chance. Miss Davis never seemed to wish to take it.

She seemed to have nothing to say. She had neither opinions nor tastes. She hadn't even an appetite. The amount she left on her plate would have fed a plough-boy—I believe often *did* feed a plough-boy; she made no more impression on the viands than did her extra place at the table itself. It was such a large table, it could easily have accommodated, besides the eight Sylvesters and myself, half-a-dozen more such wrens as Fanny.

So the Sylvester women came gradually to ignore her. They

didn't mean to. The original joke, the joke of Stephen's finding himself a wife, still aroused in them the old hilarity. (It was odd, sometimes, to hear them go off in a reminiscent gale of laughter, of which the very cause and spring sat quietly by.) They had meant to cosset Stephen's bride uncommonly, perhaps spoil her a little, as they spoilt him. But how could they, when she slipped so unobtrusively about that one never knew, without looking, whether she was or wasn't in the room?— When she uttered never a 'no', always a 'yes', to every proposal? She didn't even choose her marriage chamber. *I* knew I was to be dispossessed, as soon as I went home, of my room above the grassplot—but on the say-so of my Aunt Charlotte. " 'Tis the best that's left," she coaxed me. " 'Tis the one most fitting. When 'ee comes back next year, us'll hang new curtains for 'ee where Fanny bides now; maybe there'll be a new carpet. 'Twill be so pretty, 'ee did never see the like . . ."

If I didn't protest, it was because I knew something my aunts didn't; and I thought Fanny Davis must have said *something*—uttered perhaps no more than some half-caught words which nonetheless lodged in Charlotte's memory—denoting a wish to look out for ever on our crab. If so, I considered it highly romantic. (I was as avid, that year, for romances, lent me by our cook at home, as I had once been for fairy-tales.) —I think now that perhaps Fanny shared my taste, for as the days passed, as it became increasingly obvious that she understood nothing whatever of the female work of a farm, my aunts' uninhibited questioning drew forth a highly romantic history.

It was romantically vague. Of her childhood, even of her young girlhood, the most that could be discovered was a sort of shadow-novelette. A father deceased before she could re-

member him nonetheless trailed clouds of glory: hints of aristocratic connections at once explained and made impressive an
absence of paternal relations so complete as to have been otherwise suspicious. Her mother, also in the grave, had been so
distinguished for ethereal beauty that her early death occasioned no surprise. If it seemed likely that she had also been a
milliner, that was simply because Fanny Davis herself was so
apprenticed.—This last was the single fact possible to check,
impossible of disguise: my Uncle Stephen having first encountered her in a milliner's shop.

"Whatever was he at, dear souls?" marvelled my Aunt Rachel.

"Him saw she through the window," said my Aunt Grace.

"And what *did* he see? I be proper baffled," said my simple
Aunt Rachel. "If 'twas any one of we, for example, 'twould
make sense . . ." She turned—I was with them in the kitchen,
for baking-day, so I saw her—and in a scrap of mirror preened
her long, milk-coloured throat. She was in fact the beauty of
them all; and modestly but thoroughly knew it.

"Hark to me, bors," said my Aunt Charlotte. "There's women
catch men by beauty, and others that catch 'em by worth. Us
three, and why not speak it, caught *our* men by both."

"So far as concerns Matthew, 'twas all made up 'twixt 'ee
and I," said my Aunt Grace calmly.

"Ah, but he'd never have taken 'ee without your beauty,"
retorted Charlotte. "That's a Sylvester male all over—wants
the earth and also the moon. But there's some women catches
'em by something other; 'tis not beauty—for to me Fanny's no
more than an emmet—and not by worth, for she knows naught
to any purpose. 'Ee might call it a kind of female charm; which

I say she must possess, or how would young Stephen be so beguiled?"

"You say it, but do 'ee see it?" demanded my Aunt Grace.

"No," said my Aunt Charlotte. "But I might, were I a male."

There was a short pause. I think I was forgotten—by this time I was under the table, cutting cats out of pastry.

"Charlotte: what's she to do here?" asked my Aunt Grace point-blank.

"Trim up our bonnets," said Charlotte, laughing.

Thus good-humouredly, tolerantly, almost off-handedly, they accepted Stephen's choice: no doubt feeling the Sylvesters strong enough to afford, as a sort of luxury, this little, last, useless bride.

2

She did nothing all day long.

It was astonishing to me, in an adult. I suppose that in a sense I did nothing either—or nothing useful; but I was so perpetually running after my aunts, or strumming on the piano, or loitering about the yard or drawing the crab-tree, that I certainly couldn't have been called inactive. Fanny Davis did nothing but sit at a window, or wander about the house. (She liked to look at things, particularly in the parlour: she liked looking at the lustre-ware in the cabinet, which I once or twice found her handling, and at the big unstrung harp.) This moony behaviour took us some little time to get used to; but my aunts had decided upon tolerance, and they were also, I feel, a trifle guiltily aware that they ought to take her more firmly in hand.

The truth was that they were all too efficient to make good teachers, save of underlings who could be bawled at; it cost them so much not to bawl at Fanny—when she bungled her first baking of bread, for instance, or when her butter wouldn't come, or when she couldn't tell a pullet from a cockerel—that they tacitly agreed to spare their pains. In addition, my Aunt Charlotte produced what today would be called an alibi, by declaring that Fanny would soon find business of her own.

"They small, delicate souls being often remarkable breeders," stated my Aunt Charlotte. "I've seen 'em time without number bring forth twins like Bible ewes. Wait till this time twelve-months, bors, and see if she b'aint able for that!"

It occurred to no one that Fanny Davis possessed at least one quite striking capacity besides: the ability to seize a chance. No doubt it meant little enough, when Stephen stared at her through a window, that she smiled modestly back; not much more that she allowed him, (he, thus encouraged, waiting outside the shop), to escort her for a stroll along the waterfront; the milliner-society of Plymouth no doubt winked at such slight irregularities. But it was actually the same evening that Stephen made his bid for her, and she took him next day. She had nothing but her wits to guide her. If it is just possible some Plymouth tradesman knew the Sylvesters by repute, Fanny had hardly time to make enquiry. Stephen himself no doubt bore certain marks of prosperity, and there was the Sylvester gig stabled at his inn; his person was good, particularly if one hadn't seen his brothers, and his intention plain. But essentially Fanny had to rely on her own wits, and her decision to take him was uncommonly quick, bold and opportunist. With equal boldness, that decision once taken, she burnt her boats—abandoned her shop, packed her bag, and got into the gig. . . .

My aunts put all this down to Stephen's masterfulness; saw Fanny idle, passive, will-less as a weather-vane; and came gradually to ignore her.—I must remember that they were also, at this time, pre-occupied by a slight skirmish with my uncles; a belated engagement, so to speak, after long armistice, in the old Sylvester war.

3

IT began with a letter.—Everything happened, that summer; this letter arrived immediately upon Stephen's. Letters came more rarely to the farm than might be supposed: we had, or should have had, seven over-seas correspondents. But all Sylvesters shared an ineradicable distaste for penmanship, and if their sons scrawled a line apiece each Christmastide my aunts were perfectly content. They wrote no oftener themselves— though they, at Christmas, also dispatched parcels. To receive a letter in mid-August was therefore almost a cause for alarm: big and brave as she was, Charlotte opened it qualmishly. How extra-joyful then its contents! It was from Australia: her eldest son Charlie was coming home.

Charlotte bawled the good news from one end of the house to the other; her sisters-in-law rejoiced with her. The male Sylvesters, however, were less responsive; Tobias in particular showing no enthusiasm whatever at the prospect of his son's return. For once one could tell what he was thinking: one gathered the impression—he emanated, still silently, the strong impression—that he disapproved. Charlie's letter spoke of no business to bring him home. Except on business, Sylvesters didn't voyage. They didn't so squander their cash. If they had cash to spare, they put it into land. Somehow, behind Tobias' silence, some such thoughts could be felt astir; and my Aunt Charlotte lost patience with him.

"What all they Sylvesters overlook," observed she tartly, "is the fact that they be mortal. B'aint Charlie eldest son of eldest son? B'aint he in due course to rule after Tobias? 'Twas never a very clever act to me, to let 'un go foreign; and 'tis but nature he've a longing to watch over what in time's to be his own."

Nothing can speak more strongly for the relations between the three women, than that my Aunts Grace and Rachel thoroughly agreed with her.—It was always understood among them that all cousins together retained right, so to speak, of return. If they prospered and took root over-sea, well and good; if not, the farm should receive them back. What my aunts visualised, and I think almost hoped for, was a new-old pattern repeating itself: Charlie in his father's place, with his kinsmen to back him. They were all a good deal younger than their husbands—Sylvester men marrying late, Sylvester women early; it was natural in them to look to the future. But one couldn't put such a view to Tobias, or Matthew, or Luke; all male Sylvesters, as my Aunt Charlotte observed, resolutely considering themselves immortal.

She didn't attack her Tobias directly: she merely prepared, rather elaborately, the big southward-looking attic. She merely said a word or two in Frampton—so that Tobias, on market-day, had a word or two said to him. But she neither sought nor allowed argument, and after the first day or two my Cousin Charles wasn't much spoken of. There was no exact date to look forward to—there wasn't even a date on his letter; and Stephen's marriage was imminent.

My aunts were determined to spread the grandest marriage-feast yet, a feast to astound all Frampton. They were so busy from morning till night, they hadn't time for Fanny Davis. Admittedly there could be no feast without her; but except for her mere physical presence, they needed her no more, within-doors, than their menfolk needed her without.

4

ALL therefore conspired to make *me* Fanny's little friend.

To me, and to me alone, Fanny talked. We had long conversations together, chiefly in the parlour, where I, drifting in for a bout of 'Chopsticks', so often found her before me. I remember the first of these sessions most accurately, from its unpromising beginning to its delicious close.

She began by questioning me about my life in London, a topic which I disliked. While I was at the farm I wanted to *be* at the farm, altogether, as though I lived there. But Miss Davis' sharp little questions prodded the answers out of me, she was soon in possession of our address, (Bayswater), the size of our house, (seven bedrooms), the number of maids we kept, (three), and my father's profession. When I told her he was a Queen's Counsel, she looked impressed.

"He'll be quite in the top set amongst lawyers, then?"

I said I supposed so.

"And no doubt your mother's a smart lady? Gives dinner-parties and all that?"

I nodded dumbly. My mother did give dinner-parties; I hated them. They made the servants cross all day, cook grumbled about bricks without straw; the guests, invited on the strict cutlet-for-a-cutlet system, never generated the least social warmth.—I used to look down at them through the banisters as they went cheerlessly home, and wonder not only why my mother asked them, but why they *came* . . .

"If ever I'm in London, perhaps she'll ask *me*," suggested Fanny Davis.

I couldn't think of anything less likely. My mother's cutlet-for-a-cutlet rule was abrogated only in the case of judges. Moreover, why should Fanny Davis ever be in London? No Sylvester travelled farther than Plymouth—or, of course, Australia. Perhaps something of this showed in my face: some dubiety, even scorn; at once my new Aunt Fanny, changing her whole aspect, bent on me a most sweet and romantic look.

"It's just that I should be so proud," she explained, "to show off my handsome hubby. If *you* ever love, dear, and are fortunate enough to win the man of your choice, you will enter into my feelings."

All my defences fell. I thrilled responsively. How could I not? Cook had been lending me two novelettes a week all winter.

"I don't suppose I'll ever have the chance," I mumbled.

"Of course you will, dear," affirmed Miss Davis positively. "With those eyes, and that hair, I've no doubt you'll be quite pursued. It's only that your unusual character may make you difficult to please; which is why perhaps *he* may need winning . . ."

When she said things like that to me—and she was to say

them constantly—I was her little friend indeed. For she made me too a figure of romance—at least potentially. In time the man of my choice took recognizable shape: I decided that he would be a medical missionary. This rather bothered Fanny, because I was going to be so beautiful; we compromised on the hope that my beauty would be the saintly kind, leading men's thoughts to higher, not lower levels.—She often warned me on this point, telling me beauty was a fatal snare; more colloquially adding that a pretty friend of hers used to be so pestered by chaps in Plymouth, she married in haste to repent at leisure. When I offered the example of my aunts, whose looks seemed to have done them no harm at all, Fanny merely sighed that some had *all* the luck—but consider Lady Hamilton. Under Fanny's guidance, I willingly did so. She was quite strong on one sort of history, the sort my schoolbooks left out, and recounted poor Emma's tale with real feeling. Her beauty hadn't been the saintly kind at all, and see what came of it. She died in debt. "Debts!" cried Fanny Davis bitterly; and for once broke off her flow to brood . . .

But we didn't often touch on anything so sordid. Our conversation in general was high-minded, sentimental, and unreal, like the conversations in cook's novelettes.

We talked, in fact, just like a couple of milliners.

That we didn't talk much about my Uncle Stephen at first both surprised and disappointed me; gradually I came to suspect that Fanny herself, in a different way, had been surprised and disappointed too. I thought she must have expected to see more of him: she wasn't used to farm ways, to the two modes of life, the male and the female, running concurrently, but almost separately. Moreover, little as we saw any of the men, (except at table, where they silently filled themselves, and on Sundays, when they mostly slept), we saw Stephen even less. He had returned to his natural place as *youngest*— took naturally all the hardest tasks, stayed longest with the harvesters, turned out earliest to the cows; and on Sundays did duty for four. No Sylvester saw any reason why he shouldn't. His courting was presumed to have been got over in Plymouth, his wedding was settled; how then could his status as Fanny's betrothed affect his primary status as youngest brother?—So would have reasoned, I have no doubt, any Sylvester who thought about it; I have equally no doubt they never thought about it at all.

All the same, I saw how natural it was for Fanny to be a little dissatisfied. I wondered if they met again sometimes, by night, under the crab. I wondered if they met *every* night . . . I longed to find out, but honour forbade spying; also I was a very sound sleeper.—Just once, about mid-month, after a supper of cold goose, I did wake up at the right time—at least all the house was still—and did slip to the window; but the night was so dark I could see nothing, had there been anything for me to see.

CHAPTER IV

I

I WAS Fanny Davis' little friend; I might have been her little bridesmaid. She suggested it with flattering diffidence, hoping I wasn't too grand, so that besides achieving an ambition I should have had also the pleasant sense of conferring a favour. —But alas for us both! At last I realised, or rather faced, the lamentable fact that I shouldn't even be at the wedding. Dates defeated us. My day of departure couldn't be postponed, because of the opening of school-term, nor Fanny's marriage-day put forward, because of the banns. Exactly five days defrauded me of pink spotted muslin and a rose-bud wreath, or, alternatively, blue, with forgetmenots. . . .

When I wistfully enquired where these glories would have been procured, Fanny Davis instantly explained that she meant to send my measurements to Plymouth, to the first-class dressmaker engaged on her trousseau.

"Any way, I'll be able to see *that*," said I.

Fanny Davis laughed lightly.

"Don't you know, dear, all real lace has to be *whipped* on? I expect nothing till the last moment—and if I walk up the aisle with tackings in, Madame Rose will still have worked wonders."

41

THE GIPSY IN THE PARLOUR

When I repeated this to my aunts, I was surprised to see how little impressed they were. They merely looked at each other, for once silent, until my Aunt Grace rather sharply bade me run and play.

As I see now, they were in a quandary.

Though the news of our bride's arrival naturally aroused a great deal of local interest, she had not so far been presented to the neighbourhood.

The fact was that my aunts, in their first flush of enthusiasm, had talked a little rashly. Expectation was pitched too high. They were so sure Stephen would bring home another beauty like themselves, they boasted in advance of Fanny's handsomeness—loudly prophesying, and with equal complacency, their own eclipse and the bedazzlement of their friends. To make matters worse, such was their prestige that the very fact that they didn't at once take Miss Davis round visiting merely heightened expectation again. It was the general opinion that she was being kept back for the Assembly, there to burst upon, and bedazzle, the whole neighbourhood at once.

Certainly the timing would have been perfect; the Assembly Ball, held at the George Hotel in Frampton, would take place just three days before the wedding.—I should miss that too, but this ordinarily would have been no loss. I was used to missing Assemblies, I was in any case too young to go, and my aunts' descriptions of them had hitherto satisfied me. Almost too well: their triple account, reiterated and expanded year by year, offered a picture so splendid and complex—such a farrago of light, colour, music and movement—that my own first dance in London was a bitter disappointment. (Indeed, in all my life, the only function that ever came up to my idea of Frampton Assembly was the third act of The Sleeping Beauty, as performed by the Ballet Russe.) This year, however, I fretted almost as much over the Assembly as I fretted over the wedding. I caught the infection from my aunts, who themselves came as near to fretting as their constitutions allowed.

One thing was certain: to the Assembly Fanny must go. The Sylvester women hadn't missed one in years. They were a part of the spectacle themselves, their size, and their handsomeness, and the fact that there were three of them, made them as much looked-out-for as the Lord-Lieutenant. (The Lord-Lieutenant looked out for *them*. He used to pay them a compliment apiece every year.) When they sat all in a row, their three big husbands standing behind them, they were the finest sight in Devonshire. No doubt it was this completeness of social success that cast such a glow over their accounts to *me*: my aunts envied no one, were not shocked by the gentry's bare shoulders, (their own so richly covered), and in fact enjoyed Frampton Assembly just as I imagined it—that is, ideally.

This year they had to take Fanny.

No one felt the situation more keenly than Charlotte. She hadn't a jealous bone in her body: to produce one sister-in-law after the other, each as striking as herself, had been to Charlotte both a glorious joke and a Sylvester triumph. If she could have turned Fanny Davis into a beauty she would have done so at once, sooner than disappoint the Assembly with an emmet.

Witchcraft lacking, Fanny Davis continued small, plain, and—thin.

This last was her worst disability of all. It was irretrievable.

43

What cannot be triumphed in may still be carried off, a sister-in-law merely small and plain reflects no positive discredit. Fanny Davis, at least by local standards, looked half-starved as well. She had wrists and ankles like chicken-bones, arms like wands. She looked as though she didn't get enough to eat. And with the best will in the world Charlotte could do nothing about that either. *She* knew, her eye for stock told her, that no amount of good feeding ever would flesh Fanny up; but the eyes of the Assembly might be less informed. . . .

As always, the sisters-in-law thought as one.

"If folks declare we'm starving her," stated my Aunt Grace baldly, "they'll have every right and reason."

"Couldn't 'ee drop a word as to my cream?" suggested Aunt Rachel. "Fanny gets my cream to her porridge every breakfast—fourpennyworth."

"Us never talked dairy-maid at the Assembly yet," said my Aunt Grace proudly. "I say, let 'em take she as they find she —as we'm bound to do; and if any unkind, malicious word be said, I'm sure the Sylvester back's strong enough to bear it."

They spoke; my Aunt Charlotte acted. She went alone into Frampton and came back with a length of silk brocade for which she had paid two guineas a yard.

2

WE were all summoned to the parlour to see it unwrapped. The great broad folds were peacock-coloured, changing at every ripple from blue to amethyst: figured with a small golden sprig, and so stiff that they fell in pyramids. It came from

France, but there was also something of the East in it; and if Charlotte had been the greatest dressmaker in the world, she could have found nothing better suited to beautify a gipsy.

"There 'tis, bors," said my Aunt Charlotte. "Fanny's dress for the Assembly—and it cost two guineas a yard."

I think that was the only time I ever saw Fanny Davis show gratitude.—Not in words: but she dropped to her knees, and pulled a stiff, glowing fold across her mouth, while her eyes, (they looked like eyes above a yashmak), burned with pleasure. . .

"Charlotte!" breathed my Aunt Rachel. " 'Tis fit—'tis fit for the Queen!"

" 'Ee never found that to Frampton," stated my Aunt Grace.

"Brewers' in High Street," retorted Charlotte coolly. "See what 'tis to have a long memory. Thomas Brewer laid it in ten years back, looking to Mrs. Pomfret being Mayor's lady. But the dropsy took her first, poor toad, and he's been loaded with it ever since. He'd ha' charged her three."

"Three or two, who'm be paying for it?" demanded Grace sharply.

"I be," said my Aunt Charlotte, with Norfolk aplomb. " 'Tis my wedding-gift to Fanny, with which I trust she be content."

All eyes, naturally, turned upon Fanny, who rose to the occasion by weeping.—She would actually have wiped her eyes on the silk, had not my Aunt Grace snatched it away and substituted her own handkerchief.

" 'Ee'll have to make it up yourself," warned Charlotte. "All Frampton's busy for the Assembly. Can 'ee do it in the time?"

"Yes, indeed!" breathed Fanny Davis. (No one except myself, even at the time I thought it odd, seemed to remember

45

the first-rate dressmaker in Plymouth.) *"Dear* Mrs. Toby," breathed Fanny Davis, "I shall labour night and day!"

3

So she did; and so did I.

We had no sewing-machine. Every stitch in that dress had to be put in by hand, and the stitches were innumerable. Distrustful as she proved of my abilities, Fanny Davis nonetheless needed me; I could at least oversew a seam. I worked, during those last days, like—a milliner's apprentice. I am sure my mother would have disapproved; I doubt whether my aunts knew. I am sure at least they didn't know I worked in bed, sitting up beside a candle.

It was simply necessary.—I recall a fashion only just less remote than the crinoline: an enormous skirt, seamed, gored and flounced, gathered back, over the rudimentary bustle, below a bodice skin-tight and provocatively scooped. A milliner and a milliner's apprentice could only just stitch such a dress in the time.

I sewed until my thimble-finger was ridged. Outside, the last splendid days of summer shouted to me; I couldn't listen. We worked in Fanny's own room; neither parlour nor kitchen knew me more. We even *ate* in Fanny Davis' room—I sent down to beg a tray from the big table. I remember that once my Aunt Charlotte took it from my hands, and told me to take my usual place, and after sent me in to Frampton with my Aunt Grace. I remember also the sense of guilt with which

I later presented myself to Fanny Davis, to resume my seam. . . .

I was quite happy as a milliner's apprentice. Our endless flow of gossip—studded with illustrious names, spiced with *mondain* scandal—kept my mind as amused as my fingers were busy; the man of my choice lurked always in the background, ever ready to spring forward and revive my flagging interest. If that last week at the farm was unlike any other week I ever spent there—nonetheless I enjoyed it.

As a consolation for not seeing her go to the Assembly my new Aunt Fanny, the afternoon before I left, put on her tacked-up gown for me to admire our joint handiwork. I gazed and gazed. The stiff peacock-blue stuff showed up her tiny bosom whiter than ivory; the enormous spreading skirt not only gave her whole person substance, but made the smallness of her waist appear unnatural, the result of tight-lacing, therefore desirable. I stammered out quite honestly that she would be the best of them all.

4

ALL the same, it was only my Aunt Charlotte who that night could console me. I was mourning a little, in my bed—pushing my face into the pillow, snivelling a little—when she came to my room to bid me an extra good-night.

" 'Ee'll be back next year, my lamb," she assured me. " 'Ee'll see, 'twill be all the same. . . ."

Wretched as I was, her mere presence, as always, made me feel better. I put up my hand and pulled, as I had been used to do when I was much smaller, at one of her big plaits—for she was ready for bed herself, with no more than a Paisley shawl over her flannel nightgown. At my gentle tug she laughed, and bent over me, and gave me one of her rare kisses. Her big body smelled of hay and lavender, her thick tawny fringe tickled my face: I had once again the sensation of being loved and protected (and almost smothered) by a great golden, benevolent cat. . . .

"Your hair's like fur," I said. "Like a lion's mane."

She laughed again, and sat back, and in turn pulled at a thick braid. Then I saw her face change; she had found, among the tawny, strands of grey.

"I'm an old woman, dear heart," sighed my Aunt Charlotte. "I'm nigh on fifty . . . I'd pull 'un out, save that seven would come to the funeral."

"Fanny's is black as the men's," I remarked idly.

"'Twill still show grey before Stephen's, as mine do ere Tobias'," said Charlotte. "Females age sooner, my lamb; females bear and wither and age . . ."

I had never, as I have never yet, seen anyone look less withered than she, as she took up her candle and stood, half-smiling, half-sighing, beside my bed. The mild yellow light gilded her tawny head—gilded even the grey in it; her Paisley shawl glowed plum-colour, her broad ruddy cheeks shone to match; even her sighs were so big and whole-hearted, the candle was nearly blown out.

I left her, next morning, in such a blaze of sunshine as dazzled all our eyes. When the cart came to take me to the station she stood waving from the gate—tall as a sunflower, headed like Ceres; a step behind my Aunts Grace and Rachel

backed her, big and comely and confident as herself. A sudden
school-book memory darted into my mind: I thought they
looked like the Three in Horatius who kept the bridge . . .
My new Aunt Fanny hovered in their rear, and also waved
to me, rather timidly.

5

As I waited on the platform at Exeter—I was always deposited
there half-an-hour early—a train came in from Plymouth.
Quite a number of passengers emerged, among them a young
man whose black-thatched head so easily overtopped all others
that my eye naturally followed it.—Followed it, and was fixed:
fascinated, half-incredulous, at the same time wholly certain, I
stared and stared. . . .

There was no mistaking him, he was a Sylvester all over.
He was my Aunt Charlotte's son Charles.

If I had been quicker, or bolder, I could have spoken to
him. I could have been the first to greet him! But he was off
while I hesitated, lounging rapidly down the platform—his
stride was so long, he moved fast, but at the same time so
peculiarly loose and easy, he still seemed to *lounge*—with
never a glance left or right. (As though he returned from Australia every day—and that too was a Sylvester all over.) Just
too late, I started to run after him; he was already past the
barrier, and gone.

PART TWO

CHAPTER V

1

No one at the farm ever wrote to me in London. I had tried hard, before I left, to make my Aunt Charlotte promise to send me a letter about the wedding, but she would say only that she might if she had time, so I knew that she would not. Nor would my Aunts Grace and Rachel promise either—pointing out that I'd hear all about it next year; and though this was no more than their usual lavish handling of time, for once I found it irritating. Even Fanny Davis' oath to write immediately and at length could not entirely console me; I feared, or rather confidently expected, that she would be too much bemused by bliss to remember details.

In fact no one wrote to me. Evidently Fanny was too much bemused to remember anything. The usual winter-silence dropped like a curtain of fog between the life that I loved, and the life that I led.

2

To remember all London winters as fog-bound is doubtless as untruthful as to remember all Devon summers as radiant.

53

At the same time, the coal-burning London of my childhood was undoubtedly foggier than the London of to-day: the legend of the pea-souper, like all legends, has roots in fact. Once or twice each winter fog gathered, thickened, solidified into an element: omnibuses lost their way, horses stood pawing in the streets, clerks walking home from the City clubbed to hire linkboys; indoors, life was gas-lit and stuffily cold.—We did not, as I say, experience more than one or two such fogs in a winter; but even the intervals between them appear, (to my recollection), uniformly dark.

This was possibly due to the arrangement of our house. Its front faced south, its back north: we children lived at the back. Our day-nursery or schoolroom looked out across no more than a few yards at the back of the terrace paralleling our row: half-out of the window, one still saw nothing but brick. Moreover, to say 'we children' is inaccurate; both my brothers were at boarding-school, and I, once returned from my inferior day-establishment, did my home-work, and employed my leisure, alone. (One reason I enjoyed cook's novelettes was that their heroines were so often, like myself, lonely—at any rate to begin with. They finished as duchesses or opera-singers, with villas in sunny Italy—which was encouraging.) Only on Sundays did I take any meal with my parents; I do not count breakfast, which I took with my father, (my mother always breakfasted in bed), because he never spoke to me at it. He read the *Times;* I had to kiss him over its top, aiming vaguely at his forehead, as I left for school. On Sundays we all ate roast beef and Yorkshire pudding at the big dining-room table, when I was questioned briefly yet searchingly on my week's school-work. If our dining-room chairs still exist, one has scuffed legs.

They were, naturally, mahogany. All the furnishings were excellent, which was another reason why our house was so dark. What was good, at that period, *was* dark. Dark mahogany, dark oak; dark wallpapers, dark velvet curtains; even the most violent aniline dyes—purple and magenta and spinach-green—soon darkened, in London, to a uniform prune-colour. All our clothes were dark too, so as not to show the dirt. It was a curious yet typical fact that what might have been my one touch of exoticism—the one garment my mother brought me home from Paris—was a black school-child's blouse. I wore it to do my home-work.

The winter passed. I had nothing to complain of. I wasn't actively unhappy at school. I was rather a clever child. I never knew the misery of a bad report. Also I had a friend. Her name was Marguerite, her father was an important banker, so I was allowed to bring her home to tea on Saturdays. I didn't like her much, but she was my friend. On my other half-holiday, Wednesday, I was walked in Kensington Gardens by a cook. I necessarily employ the indefinite article because my mother changed them, or they changed her, so constantly. Most little girls walked with a governess or parlourmaid; I went to school, and our own Toptree was so experienced and well-trained, my mother wouldn't risk losing her by even suggesting a duty she would certainly have refused. Cooks were another matter; cooks simply couldn't be kept at all. (Fortunately for myself they all took in novelettes. I got on with them all.) Our regular promenade was the Broad Walk, the grass being nearly always considered too damp for my boots: cooks also liked the Broad

Walk because it led insensibly towards Kensington, with its High Street and its drapers, and also, I fear, its public houses. A cook abandoning me, as sometimes happened, to go and 'look at the shops,' more often than not returned smelling strongly of trifle. I naturally never mentioned this. Children and servants have to connive, and I was always glad of the opportunity to run on grass. Some cooks looked at my boots, some didn't. Some brought me back peppermints, accepting one themselves. I grew, in time, as expert on cooks as other children on guinea-pigs; a cook-fancier. . . .

I had nothing to complain of, but I dreamed of the farm almost every night.

I also, once, dreamed of my Cousin Charles.

I dreamed that one evening, when my parents were dining out, I drifted alone into the empty drawing-room. It was about eight o'clock: I had had my supper. I didn't go to bed till half-past. So I wandered into the drawing-room, and thence looked out through a window upon the street below.

A man stood looking up at me.

Or if not at me, at our house. He stood just as Fanny Davis stood under the crab, motionless, most fixedly at gaze. I recognized him for Charles immediately. I put my hand on the sash to throw up the window and call out to him; once again I was too late. The glass was still between us as I called 'Charles!' to him, as *he* moved, turned, and with his swift, lounging stride walked away.

I never dreamed of him again, much as I tried. I thought about him whenever I thought of the farm. But I was still too essentially a child to fit him into the shape one might have expected, I never imagined him the man of my choice adum-

brated by Fanny Davis. Charles was real, and a real suitor
would have terrified me. I did most earnestly hope he would
be *there*, when I got back, but chiefly because I hoped he
might take me fishing. I didn't think my Uncle Stephen would.
I already foresaw matrimony, even with my beloved Fanny
Davis, ranging him with his elder brothers as a silent, adult
Sylvester. I was rather remarkably well prepared for his taking
no further notice of me; but I thought that if Charles, (so
much nearer to me in age), was at all interested in fishing,
or birds'-nests, he might make my next summer at the farm
the best summer of all . . .

So the winter wore away. At Easter, I coughed noticeably.
I didn't cough enough to be sent to Devon. My brothers came
home for the holiday, and as usual ignored me. Their grander
friends occasionally lunched with us; I was permitted to invite
Marguerite, (her father so prominent a banker), and found
a certain satisfaction in seeing her ignored too. (Prematurely;
my elder brother Frederick eventually married her. It was she
who left him, in 1906, for a dubious Austrian count.) Summer
term received me willingly back to school; I got through it, did
well in my examinations, and began to cough again. Actually
I needn't have bothered: it was thoroughly accepted, it was
found an admirable trouble-saving arrangement, that I should
spend my summers at the farm.

I now travelled alone. I was twelve, and had made the
journey so many times before. By the time I reached Exeter my
ankles ached through pushing the floor with my feet, to make
the train go faster: whenever a London-bound train rattled
past, I quivered with apprehension lest my Cousin Charles
should be among its passengers. But I arrived, at last I arrived
—and there, at the gate, stood my Aunt Charlotte.

SHE had thrown over her head a light scarf or shawl, which made her look a little different; but her big welcoming hug winded me just as usual. I gasped, half-smothered, on her bosom—hay and lavender, hay and lavender!—kissed her, came up for air, and instantly asked if Charles was still there.

She laughed.

"What a memory 'ee do have! No, my lamb, Charlie b'aint here. He bided no more than two-three weeks. . . ."

I felt my heart drop. I was so chagrined, and I knew so unreasonably, that to cover my disappointment I said the first thing that came into my mind. I asked if Fanny had a baby.

My Aunt Charlotte hesitated.—I looked at her in astonishment. It always and beautifully happened that the moment I reached the farm every London-inhibition dropped from tongue and spirit. In London, I still officially believed in gooseberry-bushes, and never dreamed for a moment of admitting to better sense; at the farm, I interestedly worked out dates. Now, to my enormous surprise, my Aunt Charlotte turned on me a look as disconcerted, as embarrassed, as would have been my mother's. . . .

But at least she explained. Obviously she had to. For her explanation—which included another, why Fanny Davis never wrote to me about her wedding—was simply that no wedding had taken place.

Fanny Davis and my Uncle Stephen weren't married. Fanny was still living at the farm, and still as Stephen's betrothed; but the wedding hadn't taken place.

CHAPTER VI

I

THERE was enough in this to drive all else from my mind. I stood there at the gate, staring up at my Aunt Charlotte, waiting for her to go on. Fanny hadn't married my Uncle Stephen, but was still betrothed to him; there hadn't been a wedding —so *I* shouldn't have been bridesmaid; so no wonder Fanny never wrote to me. . . . If I set down such phrases, so disjointedly, it is to mirror my absolute bewilderment. "But *why* —?" I demanded of my Aunt Charlotte. "What *happened?*" I had some idea, I leapt to some wild notion, of aristocratic relations belatedly springing up to forbid Fanny's vows; my Aunt Charlotte's further explanation quelled it.

"Fanny's not found herself quite so well," said my Aunt Charlotte, carefully. She didn't make any move towards the house; perhaps she meant to answer all my questions first. "From the very morning after the Assembly, her found herself very poorly indeed. . . . So us had Dr. Lush over from Frampton, who bade she wait a while, before so great an undertaking as marriage . . ."

"But that's a year ago," said I—scarcely less bewildered. "Isn't she better *yet?*"

"Us do greatly fear," said my Aunt Charlotte gravely, "her be in a decline."

At these solemn words—amongst the most solemn in the whole medical vocabulary of the period—my heart, I regret to say, not only quivered in sympathy, but also, very slightly, leapt. Declines were scarcely less interesting than marriages to me, and in any case Fanny's wedding would have been over.—I suppose my excitement must have shown in my face, for Charlotte immediately added.

"And 'ee b'aint to go bothering and questioning she, since peacefulness be her only hope, if she'm ever to wed without disaster; and when 'ee sees her after tea, 'ee must mind and speak softly, for noise her cannot abide."

We went into the house. Usually I *rushed* in—calling out to my aunts, clattering up the stairs, dashing down again to the kitchen—but Charlotte's quiet, almost cautious step controlled mine. We went upstairs quietly. My new bed-chamber flaunted its promised new curtains, big pink roses on a yellow ground, and a new square of pink carpet made a rosy island in the middle of the floor. I so genuinely admired these beauties, my praises satisfied everyone. (The door of my old chamber was shut; I tiptoed past, under the mistaken impression that Fanny lay resting behind it. She in fact lay resting in the parlour.) Tea was magnificent, with all my favourite cakes, to show how glad my aunts were to have me back.— But in a sense all this was but my journey over again; I now longed only to see, and talk with, Fanny Davis.

The promised moment, like the moment of my arrival, was reached at last. My Aunt Rachel slipped into the parlour, and emerged with a tray; my Aunt Charlotte led me to the door.

"Fanny?" called my Aunt Charlotte softly. "Can 'ee see a visitor from London?" Within, a low affirmative murmur replied. I pushed open the door, and shot through.

2

ALL poised as I was to fly to Fanny's side, I was nonetheless pulled up, held a moment absolutely dumb and motionless on the threshold, by the changed aspect of my aunts' parlour.

It had turned into a sick-room.

It was a most minor detail that I noticed first: the lustre-ware was no longer in the cabinet. Nothing replaced it, the shelves were empty; and this at once gave the whole room an air, not of disuse, but of being used for some unaccustomed purpose.—Very noticeably, there was less light: the red brocade curtains, that used to be caught back by gilt rosettes, hung almost across the windows. Thus much less sun could enter, and what did missed, by intent, both prisms and andirons; in the hearth burned a small fire, fire- and sun-light oppose each other. Everything was *dimmed*. If I hadn't known already that the person on the sofa was sick, I should have guessed it at once. . . .

"Is that my little friend?" breathed Fanny Davis. "Come closer, dear."

I advanced. She was lying on a sofa. I recognized it as new. She was fully dressed, but had arranged over her knees, as a coverlet, my Aunt Charlotte's Paisley shawl. On a little table at her side a novel and a plate of plums completed the picture.

I was most relieved to see she didn't *look* as ill as might have been expected. She had never had much colour, and now had no less; she didn't even look much thinner. What startled me was her hair, which was cropped short.—In those days, I think invalids were cropped almost on principle; certainly cropping—*"All her pretty hair cut off!"*—featured regularly in cooks' novelettes. But since Fanny Davis' hair hadn't been pretty at all, the damage to her appearance was trifling. All in all, I, who hated, like most children, the ugliness of the sick, was enormously relieved.

"My little friend from London!" whispered Fanny Davis. She held out her hand. I took it cautiously. It lay in my own small and weightless as a bird's claw.

"I'm so sorry to hear you're not well," said I. (The scene was really solemn; I felt it called for formality. Of course if it had been Charlotte lying there I would have cast myself into her lap, I would have cried and hugged and kissed, and probably been turned out.) And evidently I struck the right note: with a gentle smile Fanny pressed my hand, and observed that my coming was a great comfort to her.

In a low voice, I said I was glad. There was a brief pause, like a pause on the stage.—I cannot tell why I thought of this, but for a moment we really did seem like characters in a play—Fanny the heroine, I her little comfort. Perhaps it was because I had spoken so beautifully; certainly Fanny's long sigh, at last breaking silence, was beautiful and artistic too.

"For here I lie alone all day," sighed she, *"all* too busy, most naturally, to come near! But now I've my little friend back; and what more can a poor invalid ask?"

I was so moved, I couldn't speak. Still holding Fanny's hand, I dropped to my knees by her sofa; and as she gently stroked my hair thrust my head closer, to spare her effort.—So pressing a cheek to Charlotte's Paisley shawl; but how oblivious, for the moment, of Charlotte!

"*This*," said Fanny softly, "is what I have so longed for! I've always felt, dear, such sympathy between us . . . And mayn't we have pleasant times together still—weak and dull as I am —so long as we can share sympathy?"

I enthusiastically agreed. I already yearned to do all in my power to console her.—It was perhaps witless, however—I actually made the offer still in my new, low voice—to propose playing 'Chopsticks' to her straight away. She shuddered. But seeing my crestfallen look at once put out her hand again, and again smoothed back my hair.

"Such pretty, pretty hair!" murmured Fanny Davis. "And such pretty, pretty music! It's just that a bird at the window, dear, sets my foolish nerves a-flutter. But you shall be with me, if you will, all day long; and amuse me with London talk, and tell me just how many parties your mamma gave last winter; and run in and out from the house, like a little Queen's Messenger, bringing me all the news . . . Will you, dear?"

I promised eagerly. I promised to run in and out continually, even when there was no news at all.

"Just what's said, just what's thought, will interest me," breathed Fanny Davis. "My little friend!"

I don't remember our talking, that evening, very much more. I just sat by the sofa holding Fanny's hand. Though there were a great many questions I longed to ask—whether it didn't feel very dreadful, for instance, suddenly *not* to get married; and why, and what had happened—not delicacy alone, nor my

Aunt Charlotte's injunctions, tied my tongue. The whole atmosphere of the parlour, dim, over-warm, which I wasn't then accustomed to, conduced to a mood I can only, and best, describe as—*accepting*. As Fanny, apparently, accepted her affliction, so I accepted it too. (I was later to discover the same attitude in my Uncle Stephen.) Even the changed aspect of the parlour was acceptable; its new quiet, its new dimness, so obviously necessary to sustain Fanny's flickering spark of life. I noticed my aunts' famous clock no longer ticking, its sun suspended in mid-course; when Fanny told me how the chimes bruised her nerves, I instantly accepted its silencing as necessary . . . Unless we spoke, the parlour was perfectly still; which stillness only a boor could have broken with interrogations.

So I didn't put any questions to Fanny. I still didn't want to go away. The fascination of Fanny Davis' society had never depended on straight answers to straight questions: it lay rather in questions *un*answered, in the aura of mystery with which everything about her, even to her illness, seemed to surround itself. (Might I not perhaps, in the long summer that stretched ahead, *find out?*) I should have been quite happy sitting on and on till bed-time, I felt reluctant as though it were winter to leave Fanny's fire; and when my Aunt Charlotte fetched me for supper, scuffed reluctantly out.

3

SOMETHING else was changed, at the farm: my Uncle Tobias sat in his father's place.

THE GIPSY IN THE PARLOUR

Seeing him that night at supper at the head of the table, I didn't think much of it. My mind was full of Fanny Davis: I had forgotten, during a year's absence, how ritually old Mr. Sylvester's chair, when he didn't eat with us, was left vacant. Latterly he had occupied it less and less; my aunts put him to bed like a baby. Tobias heading the table therefore seemed matter-of-course to me; of my uncles I had eyes only for Stephen, whom I was rather pleased than not to find interestingly haggard. (What *he* must have suffered! That was something else I had to find out.) My uncles, always silent, were no more so than usual, my aunts as usual conversed between themselves. But I think my Aunt Charlotte was watching me; I think she observed that I did *not*; and that night after I was in bed came with practical kindness to tell me as much as I needed to know.

Old Mr. Sylvester was dead; but it made no difference.

I understood at once. Even I had seen that for years he played no part in life: *I* remembered him only as the little old, white falcon, blinking on his perch in a warm corner. In his warm corner, I heard now, he had at last blinked out his life; departing so quietly, with so little warning, there wasn't even time to call his sons. Charlotte alone saw him away—Grace running out to the fields, Rachel to the byres, when they so suddenly perceived his hands loosen on his knees, and his head drop down on his breast, and the death-sweat break on his forehead, just as he sat, just as usual, in the sun, by the kitchen-window. My Aunt Charlotte stayed to ease him with a grip of her hand.—"So large-fisted as I be," said Charlotte, "and so dim his poor eyes at last, I do trust he took I for Tobias." For by the time his sons tramped in, he was gone.

THE GIPSY IN THE PARLOUR

If I was a good deal affected, it was chiefly for the simple reason that old Mr. Sylvester was the first person I ever knew who had died. He had *been*, and no longer was. I was also, at this time, slightly religious, with a tendency to contemplate hell; and I had liked Mr. Sylvester just sufficiently to worry, just a little, about where he'd gone. My Aunt Charlotte relieved me at once.

"'Ee and I, I do trust, be both Christians," said she. "Mr. Sylvester, by token of all him ever said or acted, was so pagan as a savage. Nonetheless, seeing what fine property him bequeathed Tobias, and regarding moreover the gentleness of his latter years, us may hope to meet he in Paradise. Be us worthy," added my Aunt Charlotte severely, "for ruffian as he was, on my first acquaintance wi' he, his last days gave no more offence than a babe unborn's. . . ."

She had the largest charity of any woman I have ever known.—Long afterwards I learned that she first supported, then apprenticed, no fewer than three of his bastards in Frampton. It didn't cost so much, in those days; but my Aunt Charlotte also dispatched to each, each Christmas, a fine fruity cake; and still held her father-in-law's memory respectable.

CHAPTER VII

I

So the summer, my long, golden, love-filled summer—the period of the year I lived by, the months that sustained me through the winter—opened again. I laid my rather shabby, rather mended summer-garments in an unfamiliar bureau; each drawer nonetheless breathed lavender—even the bottom one, which had some men's shirts in it. My unfamiliar room was so pretty, I soon grew fond of it. I ran to see the new calves, and found one kept for me to christen. I chose the name of Hercules, which my aunts found remarkably clever. The farm cat had kittens, and I christened them too, with what names I cannot recall; they were probably drowned immediately afterwards. All was just as beautiful as I remembered it, and just the same—with the added interest of Fanny's decline.

I spent at least half my day in the parlour, outwardly a ministering child, amusing her with London talk, but secretly studying her case; for it had early occurred to me what a wonderful thing it would be *if I could cure her*.

I knew a good deal about declines. A friend of my mother's had a daughter who had been in one for years. Declines also occurred frequently in cooks' novelettes: the symptoms therein described tallied accurately with Miss Agnew's. So did the causes—disappointment in love, or parental worldliness. Mrs. Agnew went to the opera, and Susan Agnew was so plain no suitor ever jilted her, for the reason that she never had one —so she was disappointed as completely as possible. With all this expertise at my finger-tips I felt I knew just as much about declines as Dr. Lush; and I dare say I was right.

What chiefly baffled *me,* in Fanny's case, was the cause. I couldn't discover one to fit. Fanny hadn't been disappointed in love, quite the contrary: she had been on the very brink of getting married to the man of her choice. (The question whether her parents had been worldly I sensibly put out of court.) I racked my brains, but found them stupider than I'd expected. All I could imagine was that something had *happened.*—But what, and when? I remembered the Assembly, on the very morrow of which Fanny had been struck down. I remembered a harrowing title—*Cut by the County.* The heroine of this tragedy, beautiful and virtuous but of humble birth, was cut almost to death. It occurred to me that if Fanny's first public appearance had in any spectacular way failed, if *she* had been generally snubbed, that might at least have started her off.

This theory was instantly exploded—for if I couldn't question Fanny I could at least question my aunts, and did, remorselessly —this theory was instantly exploded by my Aunt Rachel.

When I asked had anything *happened* at the Assembly, she beamed with reminiscent pleasure.

"Dear soul, 'twas sheer triumph!" said my Aunt Rachel. "Fanny in her new gown, so fine 'ee never did see, and young Charles the handsomest male present! Up 'un stood before all

and invited she to dance!—Which her did, through two sets
and a valse."

I digested this in silence. I knew that my aunts, like most
farmers' wives, went year by year to the Assembly without
dancing at all. They went to see and be seen—particularly, as
Sylvesters, the latter. It was legendary that Charlotte, on *her*
first appearance, had been asked by the Lord-Lieutenant himself. She refused. (She said afterwards she was feared of
treading him, he being no more sizable than a kitten to her.
The Lord-Lieutenant, with a duty-list longer than his programme, bore Charlotte nothing but goodwill.) The precedent
thus set, my aunts never danced at all; possibly they knew
themselves more impressive, at a ball, in repose.—But when
Charles asked her, Fanny stood up; and made a wonderful
show too, whisking her peacock train over the floor. . . .

" 'Twas then I gave Charlotte best," said my Aunt Grace,
who at this point joined our conversation. "Right and left beside me I heard females guessing to its price. ' 'Tis a proper
piece of Sylvester pride,' I heard 'un say; naturally taking no
note."

Fanny had in fact been the belle of the ball—dancing, when
the Lord-Lieutenant asked her, with him too, and dancing
after that with her own Stephen. ("Who made a proper bees'-
nest of it," said my Aunt Grace. "No Sylvester knowing straw-
foot from hay-foot—save Charlie, who'm travelled.") So they
came home in great triumph; my Aunt Charlotte particularly
glorying in the figure cut by her son. . . .

It was like her that she gloried almost as much in Fanny.
She had indeed in a sense *made* Fanny, re-created Fanny's
whole personality, by the gift of the peacock gown; a lesser

woman might still have been jealous.—They were none of them jealous. Even Fanny's break with tradition by dancing delighted them—all Sylvesters reflecting each other's glory: whatever the neighbourhood expected, it hadn't expected *that*, and its bedazzlement was the completer. "What did I tell 'ee!" cried Charlotte, beaming right and left like a midnight sun. "What did I say to 'ee, Mrs. Brewer? Mrs. Pomfret, what did I tell 'ee? Haven't our Stephen brought home the beautifullest bride yet?"

So they returned in great triumph. It was upon the heels of triumph, not of failure, that Fanny's illness struck.

Next morning, as Charlotte had told me, she didn't find herself so well. This was at first put down to natural fatigue; she was given breakfast in bed. But she couldn't stomach it. She wasn't queasy, she just had no appetite. This again at first occasioned no alarm; Fanny always ate like a wren. But when by night-fall she still hadn't eaten, and when, attempting to get up, she could totter no more than half-a-dozen steps, my aunts began to look at each other. The wedding was but two days off; a very poor thing 'twould look, if Fanny couldn't march smartly up the aisle. . . .

By the following afternoon they had the doctor over from Frampton. For all his cleverness—and no one set a broken leg, or a broken collar-bone, more expeditiously—he couldn't put a name to what ailed Fanny. The one thing he said for certain was that it wasn't catching; and advised, sensibly enough, a week's repose in a darkened room.

When Charlotte pointed out that Fanny couldn't repose next day, because she was going to be married, Dr. Lush pulled at his beard and said he'd better have a word with the patient

THE GIPSY IN THE PARLOUR

alone. This Charlotte naturally refused, seeing no reason in the world to do otherwise; moreover Fanny from her bed stretched a hand—a hand already pale, already an invalid's— to detain her. ("And very right and proper too," said my Aunt Charlotte. "Fanny behaved most proper all along.")

"Dear Dr. Lush," whispered Fanny Davis, "dear Mrs. Toby knows all. I would go to my Stephen if it meant my death. If I can be carried into church—let me be carried."

Charlotte and Dr. Lush looked at each other. What risk he might run, if he let Fanny be put on a stretcher and so borne to her wedding, I suppose he didn't quite know. No doctor likes a patient to die in public, especially with, so to speak, his permission. Charlotte's answering glance put him out of a dilemma.

"Us must wait," said Charlotte decidedly. "Let a week pass: 'twill do no harm. Let Fanny get back her strength, which have so mysteriously departed, by whatever clever means 'ee have to offer; and I'll be much obliged to 'ee, Doctor, if 'ee'll spread the news in Frampton as to the sad postponement."

On second thoughts, however, she kept him drinking cider while she consulted her sisters-in-law. They both agreed that she had acted in the only possible way.

At the end of the week Fanny Davis was neither better nor worse. She complained of no pain, save in her breast— "Which may well be heart-ache," said Fanny pathetically. "*How* my heart aches, to see my dearest Stephen so forlorn!" Stephen indeed went wretchedly about his work, and sat night after night by his beloved's couch. (One of my aunts chaperoning them. All my aunts believed firmly, and were probably right in doing so, that once one got a Sylvester on the proper

71

track to matrimony, there should be no loosening up on 'un.)
In this particular case, however, I fancy the chaperonage was
purely conventional, in order to leave no chink for evil tongues;
to my aunts Fanny appeared much worse than Dr. Lush made
out. They weren't used to illness. No Sylvester ever ailed a
day. The Sylvester women, unlike their menfolk, did not
thence draw the conclusion that they were immortal; what
they did tend to conclude was that anyone taking to bed must
be on the point of death.

"Us never left she alone one instant," my Aunt Rachel assured me, "all that first parlous week. And 'twas then Charlie
showed his good heart, for what wi' work and watching, and
the consequent need of day-time slumber, us were very thank-
ful indeed to know him seated beside she of an afternoon."

("'Tis my belief, as 'tis Charlotte's, 'twas that drove 'un off,"
said my Aunt Grace rather tartly. "There's naught a male tires
of quicker than a sick-room.")

For all their care, at the end of the week it was plainly
apparent that the wedding would have to be postponed in-
definitely.

Fanny could only just stand. To walk, she had to be supported. She seemed to be suffering from a complete cessation
of physical strength. If she could presently move, a little, and
eat, just a little, she could do no more. As more weeks passed
she got a little better. When I arrived a year later she was
able to be moved, by day, into the parlour. But she hadn't
regained any useful strength. She was in a decline.

WHAT the doctors of to-day would have made of Fanny's case I am not sure. Possibly it wasn't a case for doctors at all; possibly it was a case for psychiatrists. Yet certainly it wasn't, at the time, a particularly uncommon one: ladies lay in declines all up and down the country. (For example, the sister of the Reverend Thomas Leigh, no farther off than Taunton, and so practically a neighbour, lay down on her sofa at the age of sixteen, and remained there—1859 to 1880—until her edifying demise.) There are all sorts of words, to-day, to fit Fanny's condition; my aunts used the word decline. Fanny Davis was gone into a decline: they found it most sad and misfortunate, but I don't think unnatural. She wasn't yet a Sylvester, who no more went into declines than they took pleasure-trips, and had always appeared both weakly and genteel—the two essential conditions one couldn't go into a decline without. (No common person ever went into one. Common persons couldn't afford to. Also, there needed to be a sofa. No sofa, no decline.) I think that at the beginning my aunts found Fanny Davis' decline almost a source of prestige; and certainly would have resented it far more, had she succumbed to pink-eye.

I spent hours on end in Fanny's parlour. It was no hardship to me, the parlour was so snug.—The word worth examination: snug is a winter word: outside Fanny's parlour summer blazed. But because she kept always, as I have described, the curtains half-drawn, and because there was always a fire, to go into Fanny's parlour was to go from summer into winter. I do not believe I ever consciously noticed this; I felt only, by her sofa, a warm enclosed intimacy quite different from the open airy humour of the surrounding house. (I never, for example, save to the parlour, admitted even the shadow of the man of my choice.) This frequentation made of course a certain change in my habits—paralleling certain other changes, in the habits of my aunts; my first impression of changelessness having been mistaken. . . .

The house, outside Fanny's parlour, was no less light and sun-filled than before, but it was much quieter.

My aunts no longer carried on their long shouted conversations from room to room, and even at close quarters subdued their big voices to a normal volume. The reason was that Fanny lay always with the parlour-door ajar, so as to be not quite cut off from the life of the house. At the same time, her nerves couldn't endure noise, and they were so delicately tuned that even a shout shouted in the kitchen sounded absolutely in her ear. This was so well understood that if one of my aunts accidentally reverted to her usual pitch, someone immediately ran to see if Fanny was all right. I was often so dispatched myself—"Are you all right, Fanny?" I would enquire anxiously; and though she always replied that she was, she would still be quivering all over, from shock. Naturally everyone did all they could to spare her, and if I at first found the house so very quiet as to seem almost mournful, I soon got used to it. I saw it as necessary, and the interest of having such a tremendous invalid to cherish amply consoled me for the lack of familiar noise. I not only shot to Fanny's side at the banging of a door, but stayed there, as I have said, for hours on end.

CHAPTER VIII

I

THE house was much quieter, my aunts' big voices were subdued; I spent more time indoors, especially on Fanny's calling-days, of which more later; but whatever changes took place in the women's world, none showed in the masculine world without. The life of the Sylvester farm, (to me, paradoxically, so remote), was no more affected by old Mr. Sylvester's death, than if he had been a bird tumbled from its perch. Tobias, inheriting, merely became master in name as for years he had been master in fact: for years it was he who settled all policy, set the dates to plough or sow. Perhaps a little more than Charlotte he was inclined to play the despot; but his brothers were used to that too, and bore his yoke by custom.

I don't think old Mr. Sylvester was mourned very much. All my aunts had been scrupulous in their observance of him, and perhaps fond of him, in a way, because he wasn't the nusiance he might have been. They weren't at all sentimental women. They'd have been glad to have had in Dr. Lush, just for the look of the thing, but they certainly didn't regret any lingering illness. They had one invalid on their hands already. "'Twas best for he and we alike," said my Aunt Charlotte philosophically . . .

75

His sons were even less affected. I heard that even at his funeral—a most proper and well-attended occasion—they showed no emotion whatever. But when Tobias, under the eye of half Frampton, cast into the grave the last clod his father would ever own, it wasn't any sexton-handful. Tobias bore all the way in his pocket, my Aunt Charlotte told me, a fistful of proper farm-soil from the Sylvester fields.

Tobias inherited.—Even less, now, than I did then, can I understand the Sylvester theory of primogeniture. They behaved, so far as I can see, as though they were earls, or barons; subject to some undefined law of entail. Old Mr. Sylvester left no will; it was nonetheless accepted that Tobias inherited. It also seemed to be assumed that his brothers had the right of what one can only term *livelihood*. They, with their wives, had such rights to the Sylvester farm as would enable them to live upon it not only during their work-days, but also when they too should perch and blink, like their father, by the tribal hearth. None of this was put into words, still less into writing; it was simply the common assumption, directed to the common good.

2

THE only person in the least uneasy was Fanny Davis; and I found it extraordinarily touching, if at the same time superfluous, that even on her bed of pain she took such anxious thought for my Aunt Charlotte.

"Call me over-careful if you will," said Fanny Davis humbly. "No doubt it's my own unfortunate experience makes me so."

(Her mother had bequeathed her a pearl necklace: Fanny never even saw it.) "For high as Mrs. Toby rides *now*," said Fanny Davis, "what if Matthew's sons, or Luke's, ever incline to dispute the inheritance?" I said I thought, or had heard someone say, they hadn't gone abroad empty-handed. I remembered some complaint of my uncles' as to the farm being so stripped of capital, there'd be no improvement in a generation. "Grant that if you will," said Fanny Davis. "Certainly I'm aware cash doesn't *flow* here. *I* only ask myself, for Charlotte's sake, does *her* son truly inherit? Isn't your father a lawyer?" demanded Fanny Davis. "What would your father say, to see such a property as this passed about like a bandbox? So far as I can tell, whether Charles inherits or no depends first on Tobias making a will, and secondly, upon such a will standing. I happen to know that Mr. Pascoe, in Frampton, has the *gravest* doubts. . ."

I happened to know this too. Mr. Pascoe, the Frampton lawyer, had been so incautious as to present himself at the farm unasked. He wasn't physically thrown out; but the Sylvesters left no doubt of their sentiments towards attorneys in general. However, seeing Fanny so distressed, I turned, as in the first days of that summer I still did, to my Aunt Charlotte. I said,

"Aunt Charlotte, if Uncle Tobias were to die too—"

"Now don't 'ee go putting *that* into his head," said she peremptorily. "He'm more shaken than 'ee may think, to find Sylvesters so mortal as their neighbours."

"I only wanted to know," said I, "if Charlie would get the farm?"

"Sure as daylight," said she. "B'aint he eldest son of eldest son? 'Ee've come very mercenary back from London, if 'ee's set on wedding Charlie for his lands!"

—Because she laughed as she said it, I risked one question more.

"Supposing the others wanted their share?" I persisted. "Uncle Luke's sons, and Uncle Matthew's?"

" 'Twill ever be here for 'em," said my Aunt Charlotte comfortably. "All Sylvesters, I hope, may ever return to their home. Which indeed I trust I may see come to pass—my Charlie, like my Tobias, both so large and stately as oak-trees, sheltering every Sylvester 'neath his boughs. . . ."

Fanny Davis, when I reported this conversation, still wasn't entirely satisfied. She urged me again to urge Charlotte to urge Tobias to make a proper will. "For though custom, and all that, may be very picturesque," said she, "one does feel Mrs. Toby ought to be *protected. Her* son, inheriting legally, would make her position so much more *secure.*"

I never attempted to debate this. *I* knew, as I knew all Sylvesters knew also, that Charlotte's position was unshakable. Wife to Tobias, wife to the eldest son—bearer herself of an eldest son in turn—what had she possibly to fear?—For that matter, what had Grace to fear, or Rachel, so long as there was the farm?

"So long as there's the farm," said I, "I don't think it matters very much. I mean, whether Charlie comes after Uncle Tobias, or Uncle Matthew's sons after Uncle Matthew, or Uncle Luke's." (I couldn't, delicacy and pity forbade, say, 'Or Stephen's, after Uncle Stephen.') "I mean," I ended, to settle matters, "the farm's where Sylvesters *live.*"

I hoped I had at last reassured her, because she smiled.

"How safe and secure it all sounds!" said she. "Like a chapter from the Age of Innocence! You brush cobwebs from my mind, you clever little thing, just as you do the tangles from my hair!" (I was brushing it then, as I did two or three times a day. Fanny said it soothed her nerves.) "Neither, indeed, worth your pains," she added remorsefully. "Such foolish fears, and such a short, ugly crop!—Tell me, dear, does Stephen ever mention my appearance?"

3

I HAD to pause and reflect. This particular conversation with Fanny Davis took place about a week after my arrival: conscientiously searching my memory, I couldn't recall, during that interval, my Uncle Stephen saying anything to me whatever.—If it appears strange that all my uncles play so small a part in this narrative, I can say only that at the time their absence from it, so to speak, appeared perfectly natural. Farmers live out-doors, farm-women within. When my uncles talked between themselves it was afield, or after supper, while the women made ready for morning; all communication with their wives took place in their bed-chambers; the two modes of life, the male and female, ran concurrently but on the surface separate. I hadn't expected Stephen to talk to me. He used to once; but grief rendering him silent as his brothers, and I respecting that grief with all my heart, our relation was now one of dumb good-will. . . . At the same time, Fanny's question startled me, because I knew Stephen regularly visited her each evening, just before she was supported to bed.

So when at last I found my tongue to answer no, Uncle Stephen hadn't ever, in my hearing, mentioned Fanny's appearance, or her hair, at all, I not unnaturally added the query, didn't he ever say anything to *her?*

Fanny smiled again.

"My dear, he pretends adoration still! He pretends *this*—" she pulled a short lock over her forehead—"a curly cherub's mop! So if he *doesn't* speak of my looks, what more natural, when he's almost poetical upon them—which I'm sure would shock all Sylvesters to the core! He calls me more winsome than ever—dear Stephen!—But if you ever hear him say anything else, to any of the others, you might just tell me," said Fanny Davis.

This last injunction I hardly heard, I was so surprised. I had long accepted all my uncles as inscrutable; but what Fanny had just told me of Stephen simply baffled me. I *wanted* to believe; I simply couldn't. With the best will in the world, and though I knew love was blind (to me Fanny's hair simply looked untidy), I couldn't imagine Stephen so rhapsodising over it. Because I also knew the Sylvesters. I'd after all known them a good deal longer than Fanny had. When she exclaimed that they'd be shocked to the core, by Stephen's poeticising, I felt she spoke only half the truth. *Stephen* would be shocked too . . .

I was so occupied by this point, I unilaterally abrogated our treaty of sympathetic silence to corner my Uncle Stephen by the pig-styes and ask him point-blank what he thought of Fanny's hair.—The circumstances weren't ideal: we stood side by side at the paling of Cissy of Frampton's yard, and she grunted continuously.

"Fan's hair?" repeated my Uncle Stephen slowly. I waited without impatience. All Sylvesters needed time to shift their minds from one thought to another, and Stephen's mind had been on Cissy. He had first to detach, then redirect it. I suppose half a minute passed before he deliberately replied that no doubt 'twould grow in time.

"Yes, but if it doesn't?" prompted I.

"Then her must continue to wear it short," said my Uncle Stephen.

He spoke with perfect kindness. If the written words look harsh, they didn't sound harsh, as my Uncle Stephen spoke them. They were filled with a sort of compassionate acceptance, in which even I, raw to life as I was, perceived a depth of affection, and a depth as it were of goodness, extraordinarily impressive. I still, little donkey that I was, persisted.

"Doesn't it remind you at all of cherubs'?"

He turned on me his old, very gentle smile.

"Be I a chap knowledgeable in cherubim? Tell Fanny 'tis so pretty as 'ee wish. Tell Fanny all that may comfort she in her affliction—as maybe 'ee can do better than I."

I thought this over. I thought he was quite possibly right, all Sylvesters being so tongue-tied. (Fanny had evidently *divined* what he thought about her hair.) I thought that beautiful messages from Stephen, even if I had to invent them, and he was really giving me *carte blanche*, might play an important part in Fanny's cure. Without quite knowing why, I said impulsively,

"Uncle Stephen, will you wait for Fanny *for ever?*"

His great, solemn head slowly bent to my level. (Exactly, I couldn't help the simile, like the great, solemn head of one of our horses. I felt, just as I felt before Prince, complete confidence in an enormously powerful docility.)

"B'aint us promised?" said my Uncle Stephen. "H'aint I brought she here, if not to be 'xactly amongst strangers, still so far from her accustomed ways? I'll wait for she, my little dear, just so same as if we'm wedded, until death us do part."

My Uncle Stephen was the best man I have ever known. He was good.—"Also, him b'aint passionate," said my Aunt Grace, at a later date. That indeed may have made patience easier to him; certainly the wild Sylvester blood ran always cooler in Stephen than in his brothers; but I think now, as I dimly realised at the time, that it was plain goodness made his situation tolerable. He had loved Fanny Davis at sight; wooed her with all the Sylvester strength of purpose, perhaps foretasted, under the crab-tree, such sweets his brothers never knew; and at the snatching away of his full feast drew up from resources of sheer goodness all necessary patience. Looking back, it strikes me quite forcibly that I never for a moment questioned Fanny's worthiness of him. My thoughts were all for her.

I nonetheless saw my Uncle Stephen as very good indeed. —It didn't at all surprise me that about this time he turned Chapel. Sylvesters as a race were Church—or rather their wives were, who hauled the menfolk after them into religion's upper class. But I had often noticed, in cooks, the chapel-goer's superior fervour. Church-of-England looked well in a character, but chapel-cooks actually went to chapel. (One tried to take me with her; my mother's anger rose as at an insult.) So I could sympathise with my Uncle Stephen. *He* never tried to lure me from Frampton St. Paul's, where I attended every Sunday morning with my aunts; but I could well imagine that he found more nourishing spiritual food among the chapel's rag-tag-and-bobtail.

CHAPTER IX

I

SPENDING so much time with Fanny Davis, I naturally spent less with my aunts. I was sorry for this, but there were only twenty-four hours in a day, and I had a great deal on my hands. (Fanny's hair-brushing alone regularly occupied three periods of twenty minutes.) Within doors, as I say, I was constantly at her side; when I ran out, it was to change her novels. She obtained them from a circulating-library in Frampton, and got through almost one a night, when she couldn't sleep. I grew expert at waylaying any Frampton-bound vehicle—Dr. Lush's trap, the butcher's cart, our own carrier's—to beg a lift townwards; and if I had to walk the two miles back, lugged my three-volume burden uncomplaining. Because Fanny told me this was almost the kindest thing I could do for her, before I came she had had to rely on my Aunt Grace once a week; who sometimes forgot Fanny's novels altogether. . . . I remember, on hearing this, feeling both grave and angry; prettily as Fanny pleaded Grace's preoccupations—she did the whole week's shopping for the whole household—I couldn't excuse her. She should have put Fanny first.

Incidentally, this was what my own treatment for a decline essentially amounted to—putting the patient first; and I was pleased rather than surprised to find Dr. Lush in agreement with me. I had to badger him a little into giving an opinion; unlike the butcher and our carrier, he was always a trifle taciturn, as though he didn't really want my company. I thought him chagrined at not having cured Fanny himself, so bore him no ill-will, but just badgered him.

"Dr. Lush," I remember saying once, "weren't you very *surprised* when Fanny couldn't get up?"

He replied, rather gruffly, that where female nerves were concerned no doctor was surprised by anything.

"Well, would you be surprised if she got up *now?*" I persisted.

He disappointed me a little by saying no. I see now that he was an unusually honest man. (He was too honest to send Fanny medicine, which the Sylvesters would certainly have paid for.) I said importantly,

"*I'm* more or less in charge of Fanny, at present. Of course I know quite a lot about declines, but I shouldn't like to do anything wrong. *I* think Fanny needs to be amused, and looked after, and, specially, made to feel how much every one loves her and wants her to get better, and puts her first."

Cocking an eye whose expression I read as admiring, Dr. Lush gravely assured me that twenty guineas in London wouldn't buy better advice. We shook hands as confrères, and I climbed down outside the library.

Besides brushing Fanny's hair, changing her books and treating her for a decline, I also had to attend on Fanny's callers.

They were another new thing, at the farm. We never used to have callers. Every farmer's wife in the shire, and half the squires' ladies as well, bowed to my aunts in Frampton High

Street; and would have been ready enough to visit too, had they received the least encouragement. But the Sylvester women were sufficient unto themselves, among them they'd hoisted the Sylvesters to such a pinnacle of prestige and respectability, they didn't need to be reassured of it. They went to the Assembly once a year; latterly, like so many dowager duchesses, without bothering even to get new gowns for it. (Best quality silk, put on but once a year, wears for ever: my Aunt Charlotte's purple, my Aunt Grace's black and my Aunt Rachel's grey, were as known, and as respected, as a dowager's diamonds.) At Christmas they exchanged visits with the Beers, and with Aunt Rachel's family by Exeter; otherwise they didn't visit. They didn't have callers, because they didn't want them.

Fanny Davis, perhaps less secure, liked as many as she could get. When females arrived—close upon the triumph of the Assembly, the débâcle of the postponed wedding—to enquire after her health, she exerted herself to see them. She forced a voice to call out (Charlotte bustling an enquirer from the hall), that she felt just able, for a moment, to receive the kind attention. During those earliest days Fanny lay still in her bedroom—but Charlotte's voice was still loud, and Fanny could always hear when callers came. She asked them to come again. Soon Mrs. Brewer, from the draper's, and Miss Jones, who kept a hat shop, came regularly once or twice a week; and it was for this reason amongst others that Fanny was moved by daytime into the parlour.—For this reason also she coaxed my Aunt Rachel to take the lustre-ware plates from their cabinet, to serve scones or cakes upon. All my aunts enjoyed doing things in style, but not to such a foolhardy degree as that; Rachel let Fanny have

her way because she thought it might turn out a dying
wish. . . .

"Which as is well known," explained my Aunt Rachel, "be
most unlucky, as well as unkind, to refuse. So death-pale as her
appeared, poor soul!—us gave she a month at longest; and then
we'd ha' put my china back."

(It was within that same month that Charlotte bought the
sofa—or rather, made an exchange for it. Like most farmers'
wives, she never saw money of her own save what she made
from her poultry, and her savings had been exhausted by the
purchase of Fanny's gown. She therefore traded for the sofa,
1870 horsehair and walnut, a mahogany tallboy come with
her plenishings from Norfolk. It was more than a hundred
years old, so Charlotte considered she had a bargain; and re-
gretted it chiefly because she kept best sheets in it, and a little
because it had been her grandmother's.)

Fanny could thus receive her callers in style—on a sofa,
in a parlour, best china to hand. When she had me too, she
had a maid. I was in attendance Tuesday and Thursday, when
Mrs. Brewer and Miss Jones always came together, to make
their tea. (Gooseberry-wine wasn't smart enough.) Since other
ladies might appear Monday, Wednesday or Friday, on those
days too I held myself in readiness—hair brushed, hands
washed, best blue alpaca. I got no enjoyment from these parties. Indeed, it was the unfortunate fact that no one liked
Fanny's callers except Fanny: my aunts despised them for gad-
abouts, while I positively detested them because they reminded
me of my mother's visitors in London. Now I come to think of
it, it may have been just such ladies they incompetently aped,
when they tinkled with affected laughter, and told me not to

listen, and pinched my cheek with their gloves on. I would have had nothing to do with them, if I hadn't been putting Fanny first.

She, to my surprise, never seemed tired by these visits at all. She seemed if anything better, and stronger for them.—I remember with what a look of life, almost of energy, she once called me back from seeing Miss Jones and Mrs. Brewer out.

"Sit down, dear, another moment," cried Fanny Davis, "before Mrs. Toby calls you to the great, groaning board." (She meant our supper. Her guests often stayed so late, they smelled cooking as they left. My Aunt Grace used to affirm they'd be glad enough to stay for that also, but Fanny herself could endure pork no more than noise.) "If *you*, dear, find my little parties rather dull and lifeless," continued Fanny Davis, quite sharply, "that's just your London breeding. Just reflect how *much* duller we should be without them! Has there ever been *any* society here before?—Though Sylvesters are almost *County*? So I really must ask you not to pull quite such a long face again, when Miss Jones offers to kiss you. . . ."

It was the measure of her emotional empire over me that I didn't protest. Because to speak of Miss Jones or Mrs. Brewer in the same breath as County was simply fantastic. County didn't even shop at their shops. If Sylvesters wanted County-callers my Aunt Charlotte had only to pay one visit-in-form upon the Lord-Lieutenant's lady, to be sure of *her* return visit at least once every two years. . . . I didn't protest, because Fanny's callers gave her pleasure. But I wasn't blind. I saw more than Fanny perhaps thought. Miss Jones, and Mrs. Brewer, produced a little illusion of society; Miss Jones also, occasionally, brought Fanny a letter.

87

I NATURALLY wasn't cut off from my aunts entirely. I recall in particular, about mid-August, one specially enjoyable conversation with Charlotte.

It was a very warm, still evening: I, glancing from the window of Fanny's bedroom, (where I had been sent after a fresh handkerchief), saw her standing for once idle beside the little crab; and for once letting Fanny wait, ran down, and out, to join her.

(To reach the crab-apple plot from any upstairs-room one had to go down the main stair, then out through the kitchen, and round the whole west wing of the house. By the great front door it would have been quicker, but that door was always barred. It had been barred on the night of Fanny's arrival; like all Sylvester brides, she had entered by the court. I remembered this as I ran down, because I was also remembering seeing Fanny there, under the crab; looking up at the house, as though—why should the childish fancy strike me now? It certainly hadn't *then*—as though putting a spell on it.)

My Aunt Charlotte turned as I approached, and, smiling, laid a hand to the tree's slender trunk.

"Be 'ee come to portray our crab at last?" said she.

I was a little disconcerted. It hadn't occurred to me that my absorption in Fanny Davis, and my consequent neglect not only of my aunts, but of all my usual occupations, might have been in any resentful sense noticed. Certainly my Aunt Charlotte didn't sound resentful, now. But because the handkerchief wasn't my sketching-block, I held it behind me. I said, awkwardly,

"I just saw *you*, so I came out."

"So I be still worth coming out for, that's better than portraying the crab," said my Aunt Charlotte.

I cannot describe with what simplicity she said it. I think, now, that she felt quite acutely my defection from her to Fanny Davis. I think, now, that she waited for me to run, at bed-time, to her room—I running instead to Fanny's. (To talk about the man of my choice.) But nothing whatever of this showed in her tone, there wasn't a breath of reproach in it, nor a note of chiding. She said simply, what she simply meant; that if I still wanted to be with her, she was glad.

The small, the so elegant tree—the tree so admired of us both—stood like a gay and elegant friend to ease my awkwardness. I went up close to my Aunt Charlotte and pushed my free hand into hers. I didn't try to explain anything. There was no need. I could straightaway *tell* her something.

"Aunt Charlotte," I said, "when Charles came home last year, was it the day I left?"

"Sure as daylight 'twas," said she. "However did 'ee guess?"

"I saw him at the station," I announced conceitedly. "I saw him get out of the train."

"Did 'ee now!" marvelled my Aunt Charlotte. "And how did 'ee know 'twas he?"

When I said, because he was such a Sylvester, she immediately looked round for something to give me to eat. But the crabs weren't ripe, and would in any case have been sour, so she just knocked the breath out of my body with a hug.

"Ain't it true!" cried my Aunt Charlotte. "B'aint he a Sylvester all over? And b'aint he the very handsomest of all?"

I violently agreed. I asked eagerly, didn't everyone think he was wonderful, at the Assembly?

"Sure as daylight they did," said my Aunt Charlotte—with such a lift in her voice as I can only describe by the word *seagulls:* seagulls, in London, on the river, or on the ponds in the parks, being my highest simile for all that was proud and glorious. "Him showed to all what son I bore for my eldest," said Charlotte. "To see 'un dance, all rejoiced!"

I had always wanted to hear more about the Assembly. I asked now, did he dance with anyone besides Fanny?

My Aunt Charlotte laughed her old big laugh.—We were a long way from the parlour, so Fanny couldn't hear us.

"He asked his old mother," said she. "He invited I, my lamb, to stand up wi' him for the Lancers! As the handsomest woman present, said he! Goes wi'out saying I denied 'un, so he took Fanny again; but I'll lay there be few females in Devon have refused both Lord-Lieutenant and their own big, handsome son."

We didn't stay much longer. When I asked where Charlie was now, and why he'd gone off, she simply shrugged her big shoulders. All Sylvesters being so wild as hawks, and in particular so hating any authority over them, Charlie'd gone off as 'twere by nature. When him wrote, she'd a good mind to summon him back; but in the meantime contentedly basked in the recollection of his, and her, Assembly-triumphs. She could recall every single one of his partners—including the Lord-Lieutenant's daughter. "Bred just as 'ee, my lamb," gloried my Aunt Charlotte, "in the best of London schools—yet not too proud to stand up wi' my Charlie, and indeed complimenting he after the valse, upon his remarkable stepping!"

It was a pity we couldn't stay longer; she had her multifarious duties, I a handkerchief to take to Fanny. But we had recaptured, if only for minutes, the old, golden happiness: as my Aunt Charlotte stood laughing beside the crab-tree, with its leaves in her hair.—I remember the incident particularly, as one remembers a last up-shooting ray, before the sun sets.

CHAPTER X

I

THE first time I heard my aunts quarrel, it was as though the skies fell.

They were all upstairs in the great linen-closet. There was an enormous quantity of linen at the farm, each aunt having her separate store, marked with her own maiden initials; about once a year, when they needed new pudding-cloths, it was all taken out, and gone through, and regraded from unused best to ready for cutting up. As a rule my aunts enjoyed this business enormously: they had a great feeling for linen, and so loyally and lengthily admired each other's double-damask napkins, or hand-worked runners or Irish linen sheets, it was often a couple of hours before the last pile was hoisted back in place. On this occasion, to make things even pleasanter, they were replenishing the lavender-bags at the same time: when I looked in all the small muslin sacks lay empty in a neat pile, their contents tipped into, and almost filling, a two-quart measure, and my Aunt Rachel stood spoon in hand beside a great fragrant purple mound on a great wooden tray.

The scent was indescribably delicious. I determined to stay and help. Just as I was about to advance this proposal, my Aunt Rachel, turning to smile at me, with a brush of her big arm sent a sprinkle of lavender over Grace's counted napkins; and Grace called her a clumsy fool.

"Grace Beer, hold thy tongue," said Charlotte.

"Then let Rachel hold her great fist. My stars, so mad I be driven by her clumsiness, 'tis like working with a bullock."

"Sure enough 'ee should know their ways," retorted Charlotte, "only bullocks buying damask so shoddy 'tis damaged by a blossom. Sweep away the mighty disaster, Rachel, ere Grace's bed-linen also reveals its cheap worth. . . ."

I stared incredulously at the tiny palmful of lavender Rachel managed to scoop up. I could almost count the grains: a dozen, no more, and most sweet-scented. I couldn't believe they had caused the first quarrel I ever heard between my aunts.

2

As of course they had not. The roots of the quarrelling lay far deeper. But it was some time before I realised what these were: even after I had overheard, more than once, my Aunt Grace snap that Fanny should be sent away, I was still so far from comprehending that I thought she meant Fanny should be sent to the sea, to try sea-air, or even to London, to consult some famous doctor. (I freely proffered advice, and was snubbed for my pains.) The tiny, foolish quarrel in the linen-closet as its first result simply drove me more than ever in on Fanny's parlour, away from the house.

Or had I already, subconsciously, felt the house divided? Its citadel of content mind, its golden solidarity split? I find the question hard to answer: yet surely, had my aunts' abundant mirth still showered like the honey-fountain of old, I must have abandoned Fanny Davis to run out and play in it. I think I felt, long before I consciously recognized them, such changes in the farm's life as I did not wish to face. Heaven should be immutable.

I therefore ran to Fanny's parlour, and shut my eyes.

My aunts, I am quite sure, did their best to promote my blindness. They did their best to keep their dissension from me. But after I had witnessed that first quarrel—first to me—they grew a little careless, as they grew a little careless of me altogether. They were never unkind, but I felt myself no longer quite so much their pet. (I was Fanny Davis' pet.) They always tried not to quarrel when I was there, but their bickering grew to be so continual, nothing could conceal the fact that there was now dissension between my aunts.

It was appalling, it was incredible, but it was so. Only to the outside world did they still present the united front of the three Sylvester women: within doors they were divided— Charlotte ranged against Grace, Rachel an unhappy trimmer. There were days when Charlotte and Grace would not speak to each other. There were days when the quarrel flared—yet could not flare out, into the shouting and loudness that would have relieved them both. I see now how much their natures must have been exasperated by the constant effort after quiet, by the constant frustration of their natural tendency to noise and clatter. They were not naturally quiet women. But how could they shout their day-long argument, when even a banging door made Fanny ill? How, above all, could they shout a quarrel —so, at last I comprehended—of which Fanny Davis was the argument?

What at last opened my eyes began as no more than a trivial passage of words, such as I was now unhappily accustomed to, between my Aunts Rachel and Grace.

"See there, now!" mourned my Aunt Rachel—handling a chipped lustre plate above her own private wash-bowl in the kitchen. "If I h'ain't damaged 'un at last!"

"So more fool 'ee," snapped my Aunt Grace. "Why did 'ee ever fetch 'un forth, as I warned 'ee 'gainst, from its rightful situation? Why don't 'ee put all back and turn the key?"

"Fanny sets such store by the use of 'em," said my Aunt Rachel weakly.

"Then let Fanny save 'em from destruction by swallowing her conceit. However, 'ee knows my opinion ere this."

"Sure as daylight us do: 'ee've dinned it often enough in our ears," said my Aunt Charlotte—who happened also to be in the kitchen, raising pastry for a pie.—So was I in the kitchen too, under the table with a stolen handful of dough. Two inches of oak sheltered me from the storm about to break above: I nonetheless cowered. I sensed, without actually anticipating, the imminence of thunderbolts. For a moment all was still—just as in nature; then I heard my Aunt Grace, who was stuffing a fowl, deliberately throw down, like a gauntlet, her big metal spoon.

"Din it I may have, into ears so deaf as adders'," said she. "I'll din it yet again, for the Sylvester good. I'll say now as I've said before: I say go her must and shall."

"And I say, she shall stay," said my Aunt Charlotte.

Again there was a pause; then Grace laughed, a short, bitter laugh. It was so unlike her old hilarious gust that had I not known for certain, I could never have believed she uttered it.

"And who be '*ee*, Charlotte, so to lay down the law?"

"I be Tobias' wife," returned Charlotte. "I be wife to the eldest son, and accordingly head in this house. 'Twas I, for example, wedded 'ee to Matthew, Grace Beer—as 'ee was once very grateful to acknowledge."

My Aunt Grace laughed again. There was such an edge to her laugh, it was like a whip.—Yet it wasn't loud. They all, still, kept their voices down. It made the quarrel more dreadful than ever.

"I took what I'd a mind to," said she. "I took 'un drunken, I took 'un unlettered as a hind, for that I fancied the black Sylvester looks. I could ha' picked he up any day after market, Charlotte, wi' my father and brothers to back I . . ."

" 'Ee were glad enough still of my favour," said Charlotte. I couldn't see, I only heard and felt her pain. But she controlled it, as she controlled her voice. She said steadily, "Leave that all aside, bor, with the rest. 'Ee knows as well as I the thing be impossible, for whither would Fanny go?"

"Back whence her came. To Plymouth."

"To fare how in Plymouth? B'aint her little shop sold up this twelvemonth?"

"Then halt the first gipsy-van past our gate," said my Aunt Grace, "and let 'em take back their own."

I didn't realise, then, all the words implied. I knew only that they were a threat. I waited most anxiously for Charlotte to turn it aside.

"Superstitiousness belongs to maids and fools," said she greatly. "I be neither. And if maybe I care no more for Fanny Davis than 'ee do, I care much for Sylvester standing. To turn her away, so sick as she be, scarce able to set foot to

97

ground, would be accounted by all a very shameful, unchristian act. 'Twould be said, at best, we'm so skinflint as misers, grudging her bite and sup; or that maybe we'm struck down by sudden poverty, and ourselves be open to parish-aid."

So, and so overwhelmingly, spoke my Aunt Charlotte. Yet Grace answered her.

" 'Tis maids and fools also," said she, "fear hard words. I care for Sylvester standing no less than 'ee do. Maybe more: for I see most plainly, and be ready to bear all cost, that 'less Fanny be rooted from amongst we, us may pay in more than unkind talk."

In the final silence that ensued I crept quietly out, and slid through the door, and ran to the only place about the farm I knew to be unhappy in.

3

THIS was a stone-walled, slate-roofed outhouse, open on one side, accommodating a pump now in disuse: therefore no longer kept in repair, and left standing only because its extreme solidity made it troublesome to pull down. Moss-grown, damp and dilapidated, it had witnessed, from my first visit to the farm, what few tears I ever shed there.—Tears only once, as I remember, of remorse or guilt, after I spoiled a whole baking by opening the oven-door to look inside; but tears almost regularly on the day before I went home. Misery now drove me thither by instinct, not to weep but to think.

And rightly: my thoughts were most wretched. It wasn't only the revelation of my aunts' disunity that shook me, though this was quite bad enough. It wasn't only the revelation of their dislike for Fanny Davis. I didn't even begin, (pressing my forehead against the cold iron upright of the pump, scuffing a heel over the flags, cruelly scarring the moss), to examine either. I accepted, for the moment, both dislike and disunity as facts, but beyond comprehension. My most pressing trouble was purely personal.

I was Fanny Davis' little friend, and I was her little Queen's Messenger.

I had promised to bring her word of all everyone did, and thought.

Hitherto, at the news of a setting of eggs, or the sale of a chicken, Fanny had raised whimsical, disappointed brows. I now, for the first time, found myself in possession of *information*. I had such information, I could turn informer.

I felt like a person who, accepting for prestige and excitement the rôle of spy, suddenly finds himself called upon to betray.

—But betray whom? Two loyalties equally divided my soul. Fanny's absolute ignorance of what threatened made her to me a more pathetic figure than ever. I didn't minimize the threat; I sensed Rachel at heart Grace's ally. I saw Charlotte, however formidably, facing them alone. I saw also how Rachel might possibly be detached; when I thought what Fanny could *do*, the trivial conclusion was not so trivial as it may seem. Fanny could stop having callers, and so stop using Rachel's china: Rachel, thus touched, might very well veer to Charlotte. . . .

Moreover I also knew Fanny's callers to be a point of annoyance all round, as a sort of dereliction from Sylvester standards. I thought I might do quite a lot of good, if by *telling* Fanny,

I ridded us all of Mrs. Brewer and Miss Jones. In this way my informing could produce nothing but benefit.

Unfortunately I was equally conscious that my Aunts Charlotte, Grace and Rachel would have forbidden me, had the notion entered their heads that I might do so, to repeat a single one of their words. That they didn't think of such a thing was because they trusted me.—I remembered with accuracy my Aunt Charlotte's look as I slipped from the kitchen: of surprise, because she had forgotten I was there, and of distress, at the distress she guessed at in myself; but no hint of warning, of hold-your-tongue. She could most easily have called me back, to warn me in words; it simply hadn't occurred to her to do so. . . .

I scuffed at the mossy flags. (The scars so criss-crossed each other, I could have played myself noughts-and-crosses.) My forehead grew cold, and probably dirty, from contact with cold iron. I still didn't know what to do. Fanny Davis was waiting for me to make tea: my Aunt Charlotte, very likely, was waiting for me to run and be comforted—waiting perhaps with some word that would make all right again. But for once, for the first time, I doubted my Aunt Charlotte's powers; I felt that what I had heard would take as long to heal over, as the scarred moss underfoot.

CHAPTER XI

I

THE court, as I recrossed it, was extraordinarily quiet. So was the whole house; there seemed to be no one about at all. (Long afterwards, I learnt that my Aunt Grace had taken out the pony-trap, and my Aunt Charlotte gone down to the hen-runs, and my Aunt Rachel to her own room. It was the Sylvester women's tragedy that the first real threat to their house found them disunited.) I washed my face in the empty kitchen: mounted, noiselessly, the silent stair. Evidently no one had called; when I as quietly as possible pushed open the parlour-door, there lay Fanny Davis silent and alone.

"Fanny?" I whispered. "Shall I make your tea?"

She raised her head, painfully. The short, smoky fringe of her hair clung in uncombed wisps about her forehead; she had no colour whatever. I saw at once it was one of her worst days —and my heart went out to her.

"Then I'm not quite forgotten, after all?" said she—not crossly, pathetically. "The fire is almost out, dear; but blow, and it may still boil my little cup . . ."

Guilty and wretched, I hastened to the bellows. Fortunately only a puff was needed. From the logs brought in each morning I pulled out oak and ash, for substance and flame, and let the kettle down on its chain. Fanny Davis watched me fondly.

"What in the world should I do, dear," she murmured, "without my little friend? How sweet you look there, just like a little Cinderella!—Isn't the house very quiet to-day?"

I mumbled that everyone seemed to be out. I added that it wasn't Miss Jones' and Mrs. Brewer's afternoon.

"So we may be all the snugger by ourselves," said Fanny Davis. "Really, dear, if the man of your choice were to see you now, I'm sure he'd pop at once! The firelight, on your pretty hair, is quite enchanting!"

She had the most caressing voice I have ever heard. Indeed, indeed we could be snug together . . . Have I not described already the *snugness* of the parlour—Fanny and I nested before the fire? If only my mind hadn't been so distracted I could have asked for nothing more than to sit so beside her for ever . . .

"Where have they gone?" enquired Fanny, rather abruptly.

I knew she referred to my aunts. I said they hadn't told me.

"*That's* unusual," said Fanny Davis.

She was of course right. The kettle began to sing, I busied myself with warming the tea-pot. I felt her scrutinising me rather closely; I hoped she was still admiring my hair, and consciously tossed back a braid.

"In four or five years," said I, "I expect I'll have it up."

"When you'll look sweeter than ever, dear," Fanny Davis assured me. "We must hope chignons are still in . . . I, of course—" she rubbed her head carelessly against the cushions —"I, of course, with *my* poor crop, must remain *completely* indifferent. But you shall bring me your first hair-pins, dear, and let Fanny transform you!"

I had to turn my face away. She spoke with such innocent confidence, in such complete assurance that any number of years would find her still there for me . . . But in even one year, where would poor Fanny be? Luckily I now had the tea to make, and made it, and looked about for the cream. For once there wasn't any. Rachel, who usually brought up a special little jug after dinner, had forgotten. Well I knew why!—and with the knowledge heavy on my heart, heard Fanny excuse her. . . .

"Forgotten?" smiled Fanny Davis. "Quite natural, if they're all, as you say, abroad. No invalid can hope to be remembered *every* day; that's asking too much altogether!"

She wasn't even vexed. When—I offering to run for it—she stopped me, saying perhaps after all Mrs. Luke hadn't the cream to spare, she looked almost gay.

"Indeed, there may be other reasons still," added Fanny Davis lightly, "such as the success of my poor little tea-parties: jealousy often—as I hope you, dear, may never live to find—taking the most trivial form imaginable. So just pour me a horrid creamless cup—which I believe is at least fashionable—and let the rest of the world sulk as it likes. What an oasis of peace this is!" exclaimed Fanny Davis, casting an affectionate glance over her parlour. "My own, own room, sacred to me and my own little friend!—For if I let in Joneses and Brewers, dear, it's but to keep *just* in touch with the world beyond; really and truly, this room belongs to you and me."

With passionate sincerity I cried yes, that was what I wanted too: Fanny always there for me in our parlour, for ever and ever. . . .

She drew me closer to her side. Her fingers, smoothing back

my hair, offered the gentlest caress I ever knew; as different from my Aunt Charlotte's loving hug as from my mother's cool kiss. Smiling again, sitting a little more erect, she said softly,

"Do you ever recollect, dear, our first conversation of all? In my bedroom, the night I arrived?"

I said I remembered it very well. Even in the midst of so much distress my conceit hoped she was going to remind me how she had asked me to be her little friend, and perhaps thank me because I so beautifully *was*. But she skipped that part.

"I asked whether I wasn't causing a great flutter here," pursued Fanny Davis. "And I remember that you—dear honest little creature!—said no. What should you say to-day?"

This time I answered unhesitatingly. Had I not a lustreware plate actually in my hand?—And though this was but a trifle beside the changes in my aunts, and the changed aspect of the parlour, and the changed bearing of my Uncle Stephen, it somehow symbolised all.

"You've changed *everything*," said I.

She laughed softly, and lay back again on her cushions. I have said that illness made very little difference to her looks: I never saw her so nearly pretty, as at that moment.

2

I DIDN'T tell her.

Not because my aunts trusted me, nor because I feared the effect of what I had to tell upon Fanny's innocent confidence; simply because I couldn't. All children know this tongue-tied-

ness. (All children keep a great deal in their lives dark, not
because they wish to, but because an almost physical impedi-
ment stops their mouths. Children are bullied by schoolmates,
or mistreated by servants, without telling; *sooner* than tell—
since a word in the right quarter might end their pains.) I, in
my dilemma, simply found myself as it were over-ruled by this
universal law of childhood; and didn't tell, because I couldn't.

My distress of mind was no less acute. I knew that Grace
wasn't to be under-estimated, however boldly Charlotte fronted
her: if Rachel was a reed, reeds, breaking, prick the hand. It
was only by contemplating my Uncle Stephen that I was able
to hold my spirits at anything like their normal pitch.

What the rest of the Sylvester men thought, or felt, at this
time, I naturally didn't know. Fortunately Stephen was the
only one who mattered, and recalling our conversation by the
pig-styes I saw *him*—if all else failed, if he at last had to be
brought into the quarrel—an ally perfectly indomitable. So
long as he lived, he would never let Fanny be turned away.
(Angrily—if *he* was content, why couldn't my aunts be? thought
I. That his name hadn't been figured in their argument was
something I forgot.) When I thought of my Uncle Stephen
I grew almost comfortable again; saw my fears perhaps foolish,
my aunts' angry words perhaps but an over-flow of ill-temper.
(Never examining its roots: my aunts essentially the three most
even-tempered women alive.) Shutting my eyes, then, blind-
folding them as best I could, instead of *telling* Fanny I did exactly as my Uncle Stephen had urged me, and as my own
amateur-doctoring prompted: I gave her what to-day would be
called a build-up.

I expressed constant admiration of her short-cut hair. I said it looked like several pictures in the National Gallery.

Instead of persuading her to discourage her visitors, I became more than ever assiduous at their tea-table.

I let Miss Jones kiss me.

I changed library-books in Frampton even if I had to walk both ways.

I unweariedly filled my rôle of little friend, little maid, little toady. If I didn't quite fill my rôle of little messenger, it was because, as I have explained, I couldn't. I did everything possible for Fanny except tell; and if the omission sometimes made me feel guilty, at least I had my confidence in Stephen as excuse.

Conversely, I didn't tell my aunts about Fanny's letters.

3

SHE received three that summer.

I have described how rare letters were, at the farm. Fanny received, that summer, three; but they weren't remarked because they weren't directly addressed. Miss Jones brought them. I alone knew. I alone observed the extra archness in Miss Jones' manner on the Tuesday or Thursday when she had an envelope to slip from hand to hand. I knew Fanny Davis in correspondence with *someone;* and thought immediately of her aristocratic connections. But she was so honourable that when once *she* observed *me*—saw my eye on a letter passed from *her* hand to Miss Jones'—she instantly told me it was to a totally undistinguished friend of youth.

"Apprenticed with me in Plymouth," said Fanny Davis, "a milliner, in fact, just as I was, but now removed to London . . . Never let good fortune make you proud, dear," said Fanny Davis. "*Always* remember the friends of your youth. . . ."

I do not now recall how I gathered, from such a beautiful sentiment, the strong impression my aunts weren't to know. But I did, and held my tongue.

4

So the summer wore away.—If I use the winter-phrase, the phrase properly belonging to my winter, London exile, it is because Fanny's parlour, in its fire-lit snugness, presented the bright reverse of the winter-medal. I haunted there more and more, more and more turned my back on the life of the farm without. This was understandable; in Fanny's parlour life drifted so serenely, so untroubled by any imminence of storm. Without, I smelled thunder perpetually in the air. For though my aunts evidently came to some agreement among themselves, I felt it to be only temporary—directly, in fact, only towards me. They never again let me hear them quarrel outright. But they weren't as they had been, they no longer dispensed the old corporate good-humour, the old wealth of easy kindness, and for this I blamed them severely.

Naturally I thought they still loved me. I was too young, that summer to realise love can be worn away. I relied on my aunts' love for me as upon the heat of the August sun, not realising that to choose winter—the winter of Fanny's parlour—was also to choose, inevitably, less of sun's warmth; and was therefore totally unprepared for the shock about to be administered to me by my Aunt Charlotte.

I had made some casual reference to my return the following year. "When I come back next year," I think I said, "I shall bring a lot more books." (Fanny had almost exhausted Frampton library.) "When I come back next year," said I, "I shall bring a whole box-full."

"Shall 'ee?" said my Aunt Charlotte.

Something in her tone stopped my breath. I stared.—I see her most clearly: she was plucking a goose, and the white of its plumage on her blue-checked apron, the red of her cheeks, the tawny of her braids, together made up such a picture as the Dutchmen loved to paint. But the Dutch school is placid; my Aunt Charlotte's big hands jerked roughly at the pin-feathers, her scarlet was angry. I said uneasily,

"Of course I shall. They won't be very heavy."

"In any event, 'twill be betwixt 'ee and the carrier," said my Aunt Charlotte.

I was not deceived. It flashed through my mind how easily she could write to my mother and with some excuse fob me off. It occurred, more slowly, that she might *wish* to. . . . I am happy to say that I forgot all my disapproval of her, and instantly flung myself at her lap.

"Aunt Charlotte!" I cried. "Aunt Charlotte, if I can't come back, I shall die!"

—I dare say I would have wept, but that my eyes were full of goose-down. I rubbed at them furiously, and saw her drop upon me a look not angry any more. It was a look like my Uncle Stephen's: a look of compassion. But she veiled it, quickly, with something of her old humour.

"Which would be a very sad thing indeed," said she, "so young as 'ee be! 'Tis lucky maids don't die so readily, with good homes and good parents to sustain 'em."

"I shall cough," said I. "I shall cough and cough. I've a very weak chest. Aunt Charlotte, I'll die."

She sighed. She still had such a big sigh, the goose-down fanned up again.

"Now 'ee looks like a Christmas-tree fay," said she—still, I think, striving after lightness. But lightness never came readily to a Sylvester: and we both knew the moment's import. She said, reasonably, "Where's the sense, my lamb, coming hither for country air, to sit all day at a fire? Do 'ee fancy 'tis that they intend who send 'ee? Don't 'ee see I blamed, and most rightly, for permitting it?—as I blame myself," said my Aunt Charlotte. "As I do most gravely blame myself. . ."

I sat back on my heels. This was an aspect of the situation that hadn't occurred to me. I said,

"If you let me come back next year, I'll go for walks."

(The promise was more striking than it may sound. Farmers' wives, farm-women in general, no more walk for pleasure than they fly, they leave such idiocy to summer-visitors. It was as though I promised to take a cure.)

"No doubt 'twould be a very clever thing," said my Aunt Charlotte—grave as Dr. Lush. " 'Ee might also remember to cut our lavender."

"And I'll draw the crab-tree," I promised eagerly, "in silver-point. I meant to this year, only I forgot. And it's so warm in the little yard, I dare say Fanny could sit outside too, if we wrapped her very carefully—"

I broke off: too late. The name instantly re-produced a constraint. But I still felt closer to my Aunt Charlotte than for some time; perhaps I also, in my relief and conceit, saw myself as a little peace-maker. I said boldly,

"Aunt Charlotte—if Stephen doesn't mind, why should anyone else?"

"And what b'aint Stephen to mind?"

"Waiting. Waiting till Fanny's better. I'm sure he doesn't."

My Aunt Charlotte laughed. But it wasn't her old laugh, it wasn't her old, free salutation before life's jocund face. It held something of Grace's irony.

"A proper saint among Sylvesters be he, then? 'Tis the last thing yet we'm set to swallow! But as 'ee knows so much I may tell 'ee more: *I* care but for the Sylvester name, borne by saint or sinner makes no odds; for which reason and for which alone, never fear, Fanny bides. Now do 'ee run and show your cleverness before she, who'm better fitted than I to value it. . . ."

So, essentially, we parted: I, for all her anger, pretty sure of my return, and knowing Fanny equally secure of tenure. But something had been lost, as the goose-down flew up and away, between my Aunt Charlotte and myself; I should return, not to her, but to Fanny Davis.

A week later the carrier fetched me and I went home. This time I made my farewells to Fanny in the parlour; she pressing kisses on me with particular, almost meaningful, vehemence. —"You'll always remember, dear, won't you, you're my little friend?" said Fanny. "If any odd conjuncture, of persons or circumstances, should occur, you will always remember you're my little friend?" I assured her passionately that I would. I went out, my carry-all in my hand, to the gate. My Aunts Charlotte and Grace and Rachel stood there ready to wave me away.—They stood apart; my Aunt Charlotte a pace or two in advance, my Aunts Grace and Rachel not flanking her, but each taking her own position. I kissed them too, hurriedly, and jumped up into the cart.

PART THREE

CHAPTER XII

1

LONDON was autumn. The plane-trees bordering our Bayswater streets afforded me leaves and bark to please my Botany mistress. (I won a prize, that year, for Botany. It was *Cathedrals Shown to the Children*.) London was winter. Fires were lit at last, even in the school-room, and ointment laid in for my inevitable chilblains. Christmas loomed, half St. Nicholas, half ogre—for I wasn't a success at parties. In a way my summer-life at the farm made me too adult for them; I couldn't take Musical Chairs seriously. Also I was clumsy, and when I did make a dive for a seat, too often knocked my rival *down*. This wasn't the accepted mode, in Bayswater.—Postman's Knock found me equally maladroit: to one pimply youth who called me out I presented such a face of scorn that he never kissed me at all. (He complained of this, I learned afterwards, to my brother Frederick; but his father was in trade, and Frederick snubbed him even more thoroughly than I.)—The official gaieties passed off, my brothers went back to their school, I to mine. Spring term re-absorbed us. I returned to my home-work as usual, as usual alone, in our northward-looking school-room. . . .

From the time I left the farm until the middle of February

nothing agreeable or interesting happened to me, except my Botany prize. Marguerite was still my friend, I found her a bore, but hesitated to show it lest I should be thought jealous of her superior prettiness. (The social life of children is just as complex as that of their elders.) She still came to tea on Saturdays, or I went to tea with her. On Wednesdays, as usual, I walked in Kensington Gardens with a cook.

And that Saturday was Marguerite's, and Wednesday the Gardens', and not the other way round, was to prove a point of the utmost importance: since it was on a Wednesday in Kensington Gardens, about the middle of February, that I again saw my Cousin Charles.

We were following, Cook and I, our usual route along the Broad Walk. At its midmost point the Walk parallels the Round Pond; and there, a dozen yards or so to the left of the path, I saw my Cousin Charles.

He stood watching some children with a boat.—Or rather, he stood, and the children played where his eye fell on them. This impression was as strong as it was surprising: I had never seen a Sylvester simply *stand* before. My uncles indeed planted themselves motionless for minutes on end, at field-gate or in byre, but always, one felt, to revolve some problem of crop or stock. They stood because they couldn't do two things at once: they stood to think. I now received the impression that Charles watched the children and their boat simply because they happened to fill his field of vision; that he wasn't thinking about them, or about anything else. He stood, in fact, less like a person than like a tree.

Tall too as a tree. He was taller than anyone else in the Gardens. If I hadn't recognized him by his black Sylvester

head, bare and rough-locked, I should have known him by his
height; also by his own peculiarly lounging carriage. He was
the only one of the Sylvesters who so held himself; Tobias'
majesty, Stephen's looseness of limb, combined only in Charles
to produce this indolent but most masculine grace. . . .

I glanced towards Cook. She had an eye for tall dark strangers, who frequently appeared in her tea-cup. But her glance
on this occasion was turned towards Kensington, and she didn't
notice him. How gladly, if she wanted to 'look at the shops',
would I have urged her on! I was determined not to miss my
chance again, as I'd missed it on Exeter station, I was more
anxious to address Charles than ever. Because what was he
doing there? Why was he in London? I was certain my Aunt
Charlotte didn't know him so close; every scanty reference to
his departure had suggested him gone foreign again . . . Beside the mysteriousness of my Cousin Charles' presence in
London even the mystery of Fanny's illness paled: I thought
of at least a dozen questions I wanted to put to him at once.

Only not with Cook there. I said hastily,

"Don't you want to look at the shops? It's a very cold day."

Alas, so it was. Cook shopped only when the weather was
cold. On *very* cold afternoons we simply scamped our walk,
I not unwillingly concealing myself in the warm kitchen until
the moment of our official return. So Cook decided we should
do now; and turning her face homewards, inevitably turned
mine too.

I had still, this time, seen Charles. I didn't this time take him
for a dream. He was *here,* where I was, in London; I had a
great deal to find out.

2

CHILDREN are never surprised by coincidences. Hitherto, when I left the farm, I left it absolutely; not a letter, not a visit, linked my Devonshire and London lives. I might have been two separate children, each drawing breath solely in one or the other place. But when a few days after seeing Charles in the Gardens, I received a letter with a Frampton post-mark, I was hardly surprised at all.

It was from Fanny Davis. Rather unfortunately, it arrived by the mid-day post, when my mother was active. (My father, at breakfast, wouldn't have noticed if I'd received a bomb.) However I resourcefully poured out, before my mother reached to take the letter from me, such country-news of cats about to kitten, cows due to calve, as I knew she had no interest in, and which Fanny had thoughtfully provided. The real importance of the letter lay in its postscript, and in the fat enclosure I instinctively let fall in my lap. "*Post the enclosed, dear, as soon as you may*," wrote Fanny Davis. "*My little friend!*"

I immediately assumed, without giving the matter any thought at all, Miss Jones somehow unavailable: my last summer at the farm having educated me in certain devious procedures. I thought Fanny was again writing to one of her humble friends, at so humble an address she didn't wish my aunts to see it.—But the coincidence was more striking still. When on my way to afternoon school, I took out the envelope and looked at it—fully expecting to read, for instance, a direction to a Miss Smith in Brixton—I saw it addressed instead to Mr. Charles Sylvester.

The vigour of my imagination was so equal to any situation, that I, who never until that moment had imagined Fanny and Charles to be in correspondence, instantly leapt to the conclusion that Charles' return eighteen months earlier had resulted in some terrible breach with Tobias—too terrible even for my Aunt Charlotte to tell me about—which Fanny was seeking to heal.

The more I considered it, (all through English History with Miss White), the more probable it seemed. (What a smug little girl was I, sitting demurely at my desk, revolving such adult speculations! I kept the letter wrapped in my handkerchief. Luckily I hadn't, for once, a spring cold.) I remembered how curiously little Charles was spoken of, last summer; apart from describing his triumph at the Assembly, Charlotte hadn't talked about him at all. No one had talked about Charles. (Yes: my aunt Rachel said how kind he'd been to Fanny.) He kind to Fanny, why should not Fanny be thoughtful of him? I remembered her anxiety over his proper status as heir. I assumed unhesitatingly there had been some breach—

"William the Second?" demanded Miss White sharply.

I instantly responded, 1087 to 1100. I had precisely the ear, and the memory, to exasperate any conscientious teacher.

"Edward the Martyr?"

"975 to 979."

We both knew I could keep this up for ever, even dodging; she passed on to Marguerite.

—there had been some dreadful breach and quarrel, which Fanny designed to heal. What made this all the more probable was that the healing of breaches was so to speak an invalid's function. How many disunited families, to my own (fictional) knowledge, had not been brought together again at a loved one's couch!—Only the frailest of hands, the weakest of voices, sufficing to compose the bitterness of family strife! I saw exactly what Fanny was doing, and loved her more than ever.

The address on the envelope was 5, Brocket Place. Brocket Terrace I knew debouched on the Bayswater Road, which in turn paralleled Kensington Gardens. Since Charles had already been away eighteen months, I thought I might just as well deliver Fanny's letter myself at the first opportunity, thus saving the postage, which incidentally she had omitted to include.

3

"WOULDN'T you like," I urged Cook, next Wednesday, "a look at the shops?"

She hesitated. She was one of the nicest cooks we ever had; but occasionally disconcerted me by behaving as though she were sorry for me.

"I'll be waiting at the Pond," I urged. "You'll find me just here, by the Pond, at four."

"You won't tell your Ma?" said Cook.

"You know I never tell her anything," said I.

"Then maybe I just will," said Cook.

She rolled smoothly off. I remember all our cooks as having this smooth, rolling gait, as though they ran on castors. It was due possibly to the limited yet free area of their operations: a cook in her kitchen wheels rhythmically as a planet from

THE GIPSY IN THE PARLOUR

stove to larder to scullery, every one keeping out of her way. Off, then, rolled Cook: I watched till she passed through the Palace Gate, then turned and ran, as fast as I could, in the opposite direction.

CHAPTER XIII

I

Brocket Place was not quite so near Brocket Terrace as I expected; I hurried the whole street's length without finding it. I had at last to ask my way; a most strict rule of my upbringing forbade me to do so of anyone not in uniform, and even my wider disobedience—of leaving Cook, and the Gardens—didn't compass its infraction. Not a constable was in sight; at last I spied a postman, pantingly sought my direction, and pantingly pursued it.—Another rule, never to run in the street, equally hobbled me; I must have taken almost half an hour to reach Brocket Place.

It wasn't disreputable. That said, there was little more in its favour. It was a small afterthought of a street, a street of small, afterthought, two-storey villas, opening, at the end by which I approached, between a dingy general store and a dingy eating-house. I went up and down it twice before I realised that No. 5 in fact indicated the latter.

I hesitated. It was such a place as I had never in my life entered—such a place as, in my life's normal course, I never would. A fly-blown menu-card, propped between dirtyish curtains and dirtyish glass, offered cut-off-the-joint, bread and cheese, for sixpence; or sausage and pease-pudding for two.

THE GIPSY IN THE PARLOUR

Through the dirtyish glass of the door I glimpsed tables and chairs suitable to such an ordinary—adorned however by paper flowers, loud pink-and-yellow blooms. . . . But there was no doubt that I had found the right place: upon the dirty fascia a still-legible *Five* flanked the honest legend, Jackson's Economical Saloon.

I pushed open the door and went in.

A bell above my head rang tinnily; but produced no immediate result. It was half-past three in the afternoon, when an eating-house is naturally at its lowest ebb of life. I examined at leisure oilcloth-covered tables and bentwood chairs, cruets apparently uncleaned since the last fog, an oleograph of Queen Victoria still rakishly festooned with Christmas paper chains . . . Pink-and-yellow, matching the paper flowers; as though someone liked a bit of colour. The smell was chiefly cabbage, cooking-fat and onion, with onion fortunately predominating, and one could have cut it with a knife.

In short, Jackson's Economical Saloon was no place for a lady.

If I hadn't been so interested, I might have been alarmed. But I was intensely interested; and intensely *aware*, not only of my surroundings, but also of myself as an incongruous figure in them. On the opposite wall a long fly-blown mirror reflected me from head to foot—fur-capped, fur-collared, excellently apparelled all the way down to my fur-trimmed boots; I thought how astonished, and pleased, my Cousin Charles would be by such a rich-looking little visitor . . . Staring, preening, I had only just begun to wonder what Charles himself was doing at Jackson's, when somewhere overhead a board creaked, steps

descended a stair, the mirror swung open like a door, and someone came in.

It wasn't Charles: it was a woman. She was big, handsome,
dark-eyed: her dark chestnut hair rolled magnificently, ridge-
and-furrow, but her costume was rather negligent—a pink-and-
yellow dressing-jacket over a woollen skirt.

At least she was astonished. She was as astonished as one
could hope. She gaped at me, tongue-tied; which I didn't feel
she was usually. I found my tongue first. I said boldly,

"If there's a Mr. Charles Sylvester staying here, I've got a
letter for him. Please is he in?"

"Well, I be blowed!" said she.

—And for a moment didn't say anything more, but continued
simply gaping at me. As I subsequently found out, Clara had
an almost Sylvester capacity for letting time run by while she
sorted her thoughts. (Clara: her name also to be discovered
later. She was Clara Blow, and she ran Jackson's Economical
Saloon for a Mr. Isaac Isaacs. Jackson was an Anglo-Saxon
myth.) She stood now, gaping at me; also, I was pleased to
think, taking in my rich-little-visitor appearance. At last she
said, cautiously,

"Letters upset him proper. D'you know who it's from?"

"Yes," said I. "And I'm sure he'll want to have this one,
because it's from his home, otherwise I wouldn't have brought
it, but I'm really a Sylvester cousin myself."

With a gesture extraordinarily reminiscent of my Aunt Charlotte, Clara instantly twitched aside the cheese-cloth covering
from a stand of pastries and offered me a jam-tart.

"Leave it with me, dear," said she. "I'll give it to Charlie myself. Just eat that up and run along, and I'm sure we're very much obliged."

But that wasn't what I'd panted all the way from the Gardens for. Ignoring, with some dignity, the tart, I said,

"I'd rather, if you don't mind, give it to Mr. Sylvester. If he isn't here, I'll just post it."

She hesitated.

"If anyone's died, wouldn't it be a telegram?"

I said of course no one had died, because there wasn't a black border. (In 1872, this seemed conclusive to both of us.) I said it still might be important. (How extraordinarily, in 1872, even the young of the wealthy could bully the adult poor!) I said that of course if Charles wasn't staying there at all—

"That's a good 'un," said Clara—almost absently. "Matter o' fact, he's sleeping. But if I believe you it's important, and if you won't leave it—"

She paused again. By the big round clock above her head I saw I had ten minutes at the most to spare. But I also felt myself better than she at waiting. I gave her two minutes, and she capitulated in one.

"Char-lee!"

Her shout, echoing up through the open door, was extraordinarily powerful. From above a protesting rumble answered almost at once.

"Char-lee! Young lady to see you!" bawled Clara. "Says she's your cousin!"

We waited again. Partly to make conversation, partly because I was really curious, I asked if Charles had been staying there long. She said a year or so: he came in for his dinner a bit over a year ago. "But this isn't a—an hotel, is it?" I asked.

"Not so to speak," replied Clara vaguely. "Char-lee! Chrissake, Charlie, can't you find your trousers?"

Upon this less formal summons my Cousin Charles presented himself with all the Sylvester aplomb.

He looked bigger than ever. He had to duck his head to get through the door, his shoulders filled it jamb to jamb. But he didn't look clumsy; his size merely made the door look too small, as his handsomeness made the whole eating-house more ugly. Clara gazed at him with simple admiration—actually took a good *look* at him, as though she'd never seen him before —before turning back to me.

"That's her," said Clara.

It was a trifle embarrassing that Charles didn't recognize me, as of course he could not. Nor did he show any of the surprise I'd anticipated. Being a Sylvester, he showed nothing. I said hastily,

"I'm your cousin, I expect you know, I stay at the farm every summer. And I've a letter for you from Fanny Davis."

"How be she?" enquired my Cousin Charles courteously.

—There was still the Devon-burr in his voice; he mightn't, by his speech, ever have voyaged a mile beyond Frampton. I found time to wonder if his brothers and cousins all similarly preserved, in Canada and Australia, their native note;—quite likely, for if they talked no more than their sires, they wouldn't get practice in any new mode. . . . In anwer, I said Fanny still wasn't very well, thank you, but she'd sent him a letter by me, and I thought I'd bring it myself.

"In case it's important," added Clara.

Upon which, I could do no less, I handed Fanny's letter— my passport—over. My Cousin Charles received it I thought rather indifferently, and stuffed it into a pocket. But his eye wasn't altogether indifferent as he thanked me for so kind an act; it was rather warily upon Clara.

"A very kind, clever thing indeed," said he.—"Clara, give the young lady a cake."

I hastily said she had, but thank you I didn't want one. There was then a slight pause. I looked at the clock; I had now no time whatever. The interview hadn't at all passed off as I'd intended; it had in fact simply passed off . . . It hurt me that Charles didn't seem more eager for my company and conversation; he looked if anything rather willing to be rid of me. Clara also refrained from pressing me to stay. (She had her eye on Charles' pocket, and looked as though she had something for him on her tongue.) It was in short a moment all children recognize instinctively; the moment when their elders are waiting for them to go . . .

"I'm so sorry," said I, "I have to be back in Kensington Gardens by four."

Clara nodded amiably but absently. My Cousin Charles, though I gave him every opportunity, made no move to accompany me out. I walked as fast as I could to the Black Lion Gate, then ran. I reached the Round Pond just in time. I had just time to take up a loitering, patient stance near the start of a yacht race, before Cook rolled back from the shops smelling like dinner-party trifle.

CHAPTER XIV

I

I WAS very sorry when Cook left, though this too, (as though all things were beginning to turn to the better for me), had its bright side. She had been with us almost three months, and used to send me up quite interesting suppers. But my test of a good cook henceforward was whether she would leave me independent in the Gardens on Wednesday afternoons; and this one, after what happened the Wednesday following, wouldn't have.

She left me, *then,* almost at once. I immediately took up a position between the Pond and the Broad Walk, where I could easily be seen. Since I had mentioned the Gardens in Charles' presence, I hoped that was where he would come to find me.

Presuming, of course, he wanted to. I made the presumption easily. Admittedly his demeanour, in Jackson's Economical Saloon, had been less than enthusiastic: but there, I felt, I had been hurried, I hadn't done myself justice; and also there was Clara. No Sylvester could open his heart before a third party. Presuming with equal certainty that Charles' heart needed to be opened, I felt it my merest duty to place myself at his disposition.

To be honest, I thought *I* could heal breaches just as well as Fanny. If I wasn't an invalid, I was a child. Angel-children, in the novelette-world, played almost as rewarding a part as invalids. I imagined long earnest conversations by the Round Pond, I explaining to Charles how no quarrel with Tobias should keep him longer from his home.—Or at least no longer than next summer; for I must admit that the crown of my imagining was to take Charles actually back with me. I pictured my Aunt Charlotte—in what transports!—seeing us *both* descend from the carrier's cart . . . "Why, whatever brought this about!" she would cry; I hoped my Cousin Charles would silently indicate *me*. . . .

First catch your hare.

The hare I caught was not my Cousin Charles, but Clara Blow.

Or did she catch me?

I in fact saw her first—that next Wednesday afternoon, I standing solitary by the Pond. She wasn't a figure, in the Gardens, to overlook: her large, handsome person being for the time and place rather gaily clad. Gone was the negligence of her working-dress: she sported most noticeably a long feather-boa, pink tipped with black, which needed every few moments to be slung back over her shoulder in a gesture peculiarly gay and dashing. Her hat was the picture sort, more plumage, pink and black, drooping behind and before. She might have been bound for some raffish garden-party. But her gait was business-like: methodically she quartered the ground, right and left of the Broad Walk, up from the Black Lion Gate—until at the sight of myself she suddenly put on a spurt and took the last few yards almost at a run.

"If it isn't," panted she, "little Miss Sylvester!"

THE GIPSY IN THE PARLOUR

My name wasn't Sylvester, but I saw how she could have made the mistake. I didn't correct her. I was only too anxious to gain her confidence. Unfortunately my moment's hesitation was misread, with a swift, abrupt movement she pushed up her veil, (as she might have pushed up a visor), and said loudly,

"If you're too proud to speak to me, say so. If you want to walk off, I shan't blame you. Otherwise I'd be much obliged for a word."

I had never in my life been so roughly addressed. (I may say that Clara never so roughly addressed me again.) My father's sarcasms, my mother's rebukes, were always couched in terms of at least surface politeness. But however astounded I was not alarmed; I hadn't the least idea what Clara was driving at, and I saw she was upset.

"Of course you can have a word," said I soothingly. "At least till Cook comes back from the shops, because then I'll have to go home. But till then I'd like to talk to you very much. I *want* to talk to you."

Instantly her wrath vanished.—Indeed, for one truly alarming moment I thought she was going to kiss me. But she checked in mid-swoop and seized my hand instead, pressing it so vigorously that her kid glove squeaked.

"There!" cried Clara energetically. "Didn't I say straight off you had a good heart? Straight off, 'Charlie,' I said, 'that young lady's got a good heart.'—If you don't mind sitting down, dear, I suffer with my feet."

I led her to the nearest bench. It was a cold day, most people were walking briskly; we had our seat to ourselves. Clara collapsed upon it gratefully; I inclined to sit on the edge, keeping a weather-eye open for Cook, because I was forbidden to speak to strangers, and wished to avoid explaining why Clara was not.

"If you've a message from Charles—" I began.

"Now don't go running away with *that* idea," said Clara at once. She was much more at ease, off her feet. She stretched them out before her, in tight buttoned boots, and delicately balanced them upon the heels. ("Lovely when the blood runs back, ain't it?" said she.) "No, dear, Charlie hasn't sent any message, he don't even know I'm out looking for you; and if he *did*, I can't tell you what he'd say, because he never says anything."

"That's what they're all like," I informed her. "All the Sylvesters."

"I'm sure I'm glad to hear it," said Clara warmly. "Christ, beg pardon, dear, you relieve my mind. Sometimes I've wondered if I wasn't going deaf. . . . Are they all as good-looking?"

I told her, all of them; though I really thought Charles was the handsomest. ("Fair bowls you over, don't he?" agreed Clara. "First time he came into the Saloon, you could've knocked me down with a feather.") But I was by now most impatient for her to explain what she wanted with me: we hadn't all the time in the world. To prompt her, I said,

"He isn't like them in other ways, though. For instance, he doesn't seem to be doing anything, and all my uncles work all the time. Of course I know Charles can't farm, in London, but what I don't understand is why he's here at all."

Clara looked at me with something like amusement.

"Not to be conceited, dear, there's some might see a reason not a hundred miles off. You're right just the same; all Charlie thinks about, business *or* pleasure, is land."

"Well, there's no land in London," I pointed out. "It all belongs to the Duke of Bedford or the Portmans." I knew this because my mother admitted to her table these grandees' solicitors. Clara, however, was less impressed than I'd hoped.

"Don't be soft, dear," said she. "Neither me nor Charlie expects plough in Trafalgar Square. It's just, as I say, all he talks about, when he ever does open his mouth, is *land*. . . ."

"But he's got land!" cried I impatiently. "Or at least he will have. He'll have acres and acres of it!"

"That's just what I want to know," said Clara plumply. "I mean, has he for Chrissake got expectations, or not?"

2

I THOUGHT, sitting there on the bench in the Gardens, of the Sylvester farm. The broad Sylvester acres, the great Sylvester house, appeared before me so luminous with sun that even under that chill spring wind I felt August bake my marrow. I thought of the big beautiful rooms and of the broad sodded court, and of the dairy and the byres and the barns, and of the wide encircling fields whose names I barely knew. I said, yes.

Clara nodded gravely.

"I thought he couldn't be making it all up," said she. "It sounded, if you know what I mean, too kind of *there*." She sighed. "I'd like to see it," said Clara Blow.

"I would too," said I. "*Now*. It's where I'd like to be, now." She looked at me curiously.

"Don't *you* live in a fine house here?"

"I suppose it's big," said I. "But not so big as the farm. And not warm, like the farm. It's not sunny like the farm. There, there's always so much more sun."

"That's how Charlie sounds," said Clara Blow. "But if he can't go back—"

"Of course he can," said I. "All Sylvesters, always, can always go home. And Charles especially, because he's the eldest."

"Well, there's something stopping him," said Clara flatly. "If we could get a read of his letters we might know what, but I've been through his pockets time and time again." (I don't know why Clara Blow never shocked me. In my own circle, to read another person's letters, without permission, was considered unpardonable. Unless of course the person was a child: any adult could read any child's letter without asking. There was something childlike about Clara Blow: perhaps I unconsciously reversed the law in her favour.) "He just tells me to mind my own business," continued Clara sombrely, "but if you want to know what I *think*—"

She broke off. At that intensely interesting moment, she ceased to speak.—A hand descended on my scruff: Cook had taken us from the rear. She was so furious she didn't say a word, simply caught me by the collar of my jacket and hauled me round the end of the bench, and marched me away. From the tail of my eye I caught the outraged fling of a feather-boa; but Clara, to my gratitude, equally restrained her tongue. We marched, Cook and I, in strenuous silence all the way home, she breathing trifle as a dragon breathes fire. As we neared our door I did try, nervously, to explain that it was all right: I remember advancing the blanket-defence that I was sure I hadn't caught anything. Cook cut me short.

THE GIPSY IN THE PARLOUR

"The impudence of it!" she snorted. "The bare-faced impudence!—The likes of *her!*"

Entirely I think from a sense of guilt she gave notice next day. As I say, this turned out all for the best, since I do not believe she would ever have left me alone in the Gardens again; whereas her successor had a close friend attached to Knightsbridge Police station.

CHAPTER XV

I

WHEN in 1905 my brother Frederick's daughter Cherry was discovered to be spending her Thursday afternoons not at the National Gallery copying Old Masters, but in the embraces of a shipping-agent, I was the only member of the family unsurprised. This was not because I knew Cherry particularly well, but because I remembered my own Wednesdays thirty years earlier. I knew from experience how easy it was for any well-brought-up young person to lead a double life. Certainly Cherry's behaviour was far worse, she had to marry the shipping-agent almost immediately; but I think my own mother would have been scarcely less horrified than was Marguerite, to know me spending *my* afternoons with Clara Blow.

A child hand-in-glove with servants, a child willing to *connive*, enjoys more liberty than parents suspect.

I had only one period of freedom—Wednesday afternoon; but it was complete. I didn't ask Cook where *she* went, and she didn't ask me. So long as she found me by the Pond at four, from two-thirty until then I was free as a Pond sea-gull. I had an hour and a half, I had ninety-five minutes, to spend as I, unquestioned, wished; and I spent them in Jackson's Economical Saloon.

Clara would never meet me in the Gardens again, on account of her feet. I at first thought her still put out by the rough termination to our conversation there—to apologize for which I hurried back to Brocket Place the first Wednesday after we changed cooks. Later, I found that she truly detested walking as much as any countrywoman. (It was the measure of her anxiety to find me again that she had actually struggled to the Gardens every afternoon for a week.) So though I assured her that Cook was now another one, Clara still refused to come out; and instead gave me a standing invitation to visit Jackson's as often as I could, and eat whatever I liked.

I grew very fond of Jackson's. Jackson's became my London equivalent of the farm. As the Spring term wore away, and the boring, featureless spring-vacation, I found there, in Clara, something of my aunt's old joviality. Her loud cheerful voice, her loud easy laughter, reminded me of Charlotte. She was also about the same size. (I always felt people in London too small. My father was distinguished, my mother elegant, but I never admired their looks.) Though I rarely ate more than an occasional bun, the sheer quantity of food about, and Clara's lavish attitude to it, produced a farm-like sense of plenty.—Whether Clara ever put a halfpenny in the till, or whether we were both indebted to Mr. Isaacs, I didn't enquire. I looked on the Saloon as Clara's private property. I never, naturally, in the middle of the afternoon, saw it under its commercial aspect.

I grew very fond of Jackson's, and I grew very fond of Clara. I couldn't grow fond, or fonder than I already was, of my Cousin Charles, because I never saw him.

He was always asleep. He slept through all the afternoon.

THE GIPSY IN THE PARLOUR

(The day I saw him in the Gardens Clara could calculate as the seventh of February, when they had the exterminator in.) But I didn't miss him so much as might have been expected, because Clara and I had so much to talk about.

Our theme was the farm.—I cannot express what a luxury it was to have such an audience: no one at home wanted to hear about the farm at all. Clara loved every detail. "Tell again about the linen," she would say; or, "Tell again about the dairy" —or about the pigs, or the poultry, or baking-day. She had indeed an inherited taste for such matters: though Cockney-born and bred, she nonetheless recalled Norfolk grandparents—had never seen them, but remembered, from extreme youth, Christmas turkeys of such fabulous proportions, infant Blows feasted for days . . . Thus she saw the country as I did, through glasses perhaps too rosy; acknowledging that my aunts must work for six, added that work hurt no one, so long as you had elbow-room. She had a way, as she said this, (our conversation early fell into a sort of ritual, we were always saying the same things to each other), of opening her big shoulders in a gesture of frustrated power.—She was really strong. She often wiped plates clean in two, and I once saw her twist the back off a bentwood chair, just giving it a polish. *I* was only surprised there weren't more breakages, considering the size of Clara Blow, and the size of Jackson's Economical Saloon.

No wonder, I thought, she yearned for elbow-room; I thought she would like the farm very much for its spaciousness alone. I thought it would be only fair, after all her kindness to him, if Charles invited her there for a holiday. But when I put this notion to Clara, she received it with a mixture of wistfulness and doubt.

"Christ, dear, there's nothing I'd like better," said she. (I had long ceased to notice Clara's language. At first she tried to censor it, but the difficulty was that she didn't notice it either. *I* should have found it equally hard never to say, 'Oh.') "I'd go like a shot," said Clara, "and let old Isaacs do his worst. But it ain't up to me, it's up to Charlie. I couldn't hardly go without him, could I, now?"

"But he's got to go home *some*time," I insisted. "And I'm sure he must want to."

"There's something keeping him away," repeated Clara darkly.

This was of course obvious. All I learnt of Charlie's life in London convinced me that he must at least be very bored there. According to Clara, he spent his mornings, vaguely, in giving her a hand: in the afternoon, as though to scamp up time, he slept: in the evening, when Jackson's did most of its business, lent Clara a hand again. I understood him naturally wishing to repay her hospitality: but did he actually wait, hand up sausage-and-mash and saveloys, like a waiter, from the kitchen door? I could hardly believe it. I couldn't imagine a Sylvester so lowering himself. If any one bade Tobias or Matthew or Luke carry plates, only wreckage, I felt, could ensue . . . I was extremely relieved, I remember, to find Charlie's role in fact that of chucker-out. Jackson's was respectable, so to speak, only ideally; some of its patrons from Notting Hill inclined to the hooligan; and Clara told me that nothing stopped a row quicker than the sudden appearance of my Cousin Charles. "He's as good as the police," said Clara. "Better, you might say, 'cause coppers they know have to face a magistrate. Charlie they don't know what he might do. He did just throw one chap out for me," said Clara reminiscently, "which a cabby took to hospital on spec. We had a whip-round for the fare, but I don't think he made much more. . . ."

I told Clara I thought Charles had had a quarrel with Tobias, the summer he came back from Australia. I said I was sure he had, because there couldn't be any other reason for his staying away. And I added that I didn't think the trouble would last much longer, because there was some one at the farm, my dear Fanny Davis, trying to cure it.

"I've always known there was someone wrote," agreed Clara, less cheerfully than I expected. "Till you turned up I thought maybe it was his Ma. I'd have thought Miss Davis was too sick to bother."

I never could make Clara understand the exact nature of a decline. She had no feeling for the pathos and beauty of in-validism—possibly because she never read novelettes. Her fa-vourite recreation was a good stirring melodrama, she knew *Sweeny Tod the Demon Barber of Fleet Street* almost by heart; so perhaps naturally declines weren't eventful enough for her, and she soon grew tired of hearing about Fanny's. She now inclined to shrug off Fanny's good offices altogether, saying her letters if anything seemed to put Charlie out, she, Clara, thought he'd sooner be without them. "But *he* must have writ-ten first!" I protested. "Or how would Fanny know his ad-dress? He must have written to her through Miss Jones, *asking* her to help him; and if you knew how Sylvesters hate writing, you'd see how in earnest he is." Clara, still looking dubious, said *he* said he'd written for shirts. He'd left his best shirts behind. "Really, Clara, that's nonsense," I retorted. "If he'd just wanted his shirts, he'd have written to Charlotte." "All right, ask *him*," said Clara darkly. "What he told *me* was, letters upset his Ma proper; so he wrote by Miss Jones to Miss Davis to send 'em on."

When I considered this, I saw it possible. I didn't see Charlie believing his mother quite so nerveless as he pretended, but I could see him reluctant, the quarrel with Tobias still unresolved, to admit himself no farther off than London. Sylvesters in argument with their sires went to Australia: a withdrawal of no more than three hundred miles might look like weakness. It was a matter of pride—and so too, I thought, was his anxiety for shirts, they just afforded a face-saving pretext for opening negotiations. . . .

"Anyway, they never got here," added Clara gloomily.

"Well, of course one sees why *that* was," I returned impatiently. "If he wanted everything kept so secret, how could Fanny ask for them? I know where Charlie's shirts are this minute—in the bottom bureau-drawer in my room."

"That's something," said Clara.

"*And*," I continued firmly, "though Charlie mayn't like getting Fanny's letters, that's quite obviously because she's telling him he's got to apologise. After all, Uncle Tobias is his father, *he'll* never apologise first; but all Sylvesters are stubborn as rocks, so it's taking Charlie a long time to come round."

"Maybe," sighed Clara Blow. "Maybe you're right . . . One thing I do know; I wouldn't let a 'Sorry, Dad,' keep *me* away."

"You aren't a Sylvester," said I.

2

But how readily she might become one!

When this notion first struck me, it seemed so obvious that I wondered I hadn't thought of it sooner. (I had been *feeling* for it: when I suggested a holiday at the farm for her.) Clara was from every point of view a natural Sylvester woman. She was the right size and shape, her handsomeness made exactly the right hit-you-in-the-eye impact, and she had the right temperament. She wasn't afraid of work, she was sociable, genial and forthright; and she had moreover for nearly two years successfully coped with a Sylvester male.

"Oh, Clara," cried I impulsively, "why don't you and Charlie get married?"

She didn't say a word. I at first thought she was too much surprised—we had actually been discussing, when this cry burst up from my subconscious, the ideal menu for a Harvest Festival Sunday dinner. "Would chitterlings be too common?" Clara had just asked, when out I burst . . .

She didn't say a word. She simply stood, her lips tightly closed against speech, her hands locked before her on Jackson's counter, while the tears over-filled her eyes and trickled slowly down her cheeks. Because I was a child, I understood. She was crying as I sometimes cried, because I wanted something so badly.

I had to go, it was time. A child has liberty only within limits. Clara's eyes, even tear-filled, directed mine towards the clock. I speechlessly nodded to her, and ran out.

143

CHAPTER XVI

I

I was an officious child, I was an interfering child: also, I hope, an affectionate one. By this time I loved Clara Blow almost as I loved my aunts. All through that summer term I devoted so much thought to her happiness, I came out at the end only seventh instead of first in class.

I cannot say I didn't enjoy worrying about Clara. I did. To do so gave me a feeling of adult importance; doubled the interest of my already double life, enlarged my secret rôle of little peace-maker to include that of little match-maker also. Yet what could I *do*? (I was always eager to do something: about anything. When the kitchen-chimney caught fire I had to be retrieved by Frederick from the local fire-station—Cook having successfully employed a pail of water. We might nonetheless have been burnt to cinders. When a telegram came for my father, and there was no one else at home, I took a cab to his chambers: I happened to interrupt an important conference, and the telegram merely cancelled a dinner-engagement. It might have called him to a parent's death-bed. I never got credit for my good intentions, but I never learnt.) I never learnt, and I loved Clara Blow; and Wednesday after Wednesday, together we revolved plans.

We had to leave Charlie out of them—except, of course, at the point when he would essentially be *in*. For Charlie, in London, was displaying to an exaggerated degree, (almost as though asserting his birth-right), the country-Sylvester characteristic of letting no one know what he thought. We had to deal with him as an X, an unknown quantity.—Here Clara again, though at the same time I couldn't realise it, showed herself specially fitted for Sylvester-hood. She and Charlie were in fact living man-and-wife, and had done for nearly two years. So far as concerned marriage, she saw this neither for nor against. She didn't know what Charlie thought. When I hopefully suggested that he must be very fond of her, she said, Well, yes, time to time he was all right; but he wasn't a chap to put himself out; if anyone ever did get round to putting the banns up, it wouldn't be Charlie. . . .

This observation from experience at least enabled us to clear a good deal of ground. We both agreed that if Charlie was married already, in Australia for instance, whoever landed him must have possessed such extraordinary, fixed resolution, she would have never allowed him to stray back home without her. As Clara rightly observed, catch a fish like Charlie, you didn't throw him back.

We therefore presumed him legally free to wed, which was something. But the next, or shot-gun, phase of our planning met a serious obstacle. When I asked Clara, hadn't she any relations, she shook her head.

"If you mean any who'd speak for me, and bring Charlie up to scratch—no," said Clara Blow flatly. "Grandpa who sent us the turkeys I dare say might have; but he's pushing up the daisies long since. And as to my own Dad and Ma, if living they're best kept out of it. The reason you see me so decent as I am to-day," said Clara, without rancour, "is that I skipped from home at thirteen. . . ."

I was never shocked by Clara Blow. Perhaps I ought to have been, myself so well brought up. The fact remains that whatever she told me of parental negligence—worse still, of parental ill-usage; and I once saw a deep, belt-buckle scar on her shoulder—I was never shocked by, I always loved Clara Blow.

Thus it looked as though any relations brought into play would have to be Charlie's: we should have to start from the other end, from the farm. *I* should have to start. Clara, obviously, could not.

Should I write a letter?—and if so, to whom?

The writing of a letter is to a child a highly important act. Children do not drop notes. I had never, for example, written back to Fanny Davis. I couldn't because I had too much to tell her. Should I write then to Charlotte? There was the same objection; moreover even my assurance failed before the scheme of baldly proposing to her a daughter-in-law she had never even heard of.

" 'Specially if she don't know Charlie dead or alive," added Clara.

I said she probably thought him alive, only in Australia. Admittedly it made another difficulty. There really *was* too much to write; good as I was at English composition, I felt here a subject beyond my powers.—For one daft moment I even wondered whether it couldn't be *set* as a composition; we were often invited to suggest topics, and if the whole class had to compose—"Letter to a Mother Breaking the News of her Son's Engagement"—I might garner useful hints. But I saw at once it

wouldn't do. It was too unacademic. Even Marguerite's one
mild attempt at realism—"Letter to a Dressmaker Saying Where
It Doesn't Fit"—had been turned down with contumely. The
pattern-subject was "My Pet."

In the end we decided—for summer approached as we de-
liberated—that I should wait till I got back to the farm, and
there open the matter by word of mouth: present Clara as a
friend of my own, who would very much enjoy a country holiday: and leave the rest to Charlotte. I felt we could do this
quite safely. My Aunt Charlotte was hospitable as mother-
earth, she would certainly ask Clara immediately; and having
once seen her, would I felt sure snap her up just as she snapped
up Grace Beer and my Aunt Rachel. Charlie would then have
to come home to be married—here my imagination easily
jumped an awkward fence or two—and who but I, in pink
muslin, should follow the bridal pair?

Unless I wore blue, with forgetmenots.

We contemplated this charming picture, Clara Blow and I,
for hours on end. As I say, it didn't in the least trouble her
that her groom cut so passive a figure therein: country-wise
again, she frankly accepted the fact that most marriages were
made up by women. (So they were in my own world, but dis-
guisedly. Marguerite's mother and mine, after giving Marguerite and Frederick every encouragement to fall in love,
received the official intimation that they had done so with tears
of surprise.) Clara was simply more frank. She was frank—
how rarely in a woman of her generation!—even in speech:
employing no more than my mother's well-bred language of
sentiment the novelette-talk of Fanny Davis.—She never, for
example, spoke of stealing into Charlotte's heart: she just said

she hoped Charlotte would take to her, 'specially after seeing her muscle. Nor was Charles ever 'dear Charlie' to her, as my Uncle Stephen was always 'dear Stephen' to Fanny Davis; when Clara spoke of *him* it was often almost belligerently. She promised to handle him. But there could be no doubt in the world of her thorough intent to make a good wife, and a good Sylvester; and I for my part felt I could do all Sylvesters no better turn, than to promote Clara Blow amongst them.

Here at least I made no mistake. Clara Blow, despite her habit of swearing, was among the nicest women I have ever known.

She suggested one variation to my plan, which I agreed to. She felt her position would be altogether stronger if on her arrival at the farm she found Charles already there. She felt, she said, it would kind of break the ice for her if when I mentioned my London friend, Charlie spoke up to acknowledge her his friend also. "Which I dare say would take a good hack on the shin, dear," said Clara, "but still worth trying. . ."

I agreed all the more readily that I still cherished—if now as but a detail in the broader masterpiece—the incident of my descent from the carrier's cart in Charlie's company. (My Aunt Charlotte's astonishment, my own central place in the composition.) I therefore, on the last Wednesday before school broke up, with Clara's connivance, tackled Charlie alone.

2

It was deceptively easy. When I panted into Jackson's, Clara wasn't there. No one was there. I pushed the door back and forth until the jangling of the bell brought Charlie from above. Even in trousers and singlet he was still extraordinarily impressive; and even half-asleep, (though he didn't look particularly pleased to see me), still courteous.

" 'Seems Clara be abroad," said he. "Her'll be sorry to miss 'ee; but 'ee've no call to wait."

I sat down. He was so enormous, I felt not exactly safer, but more out of harm's way, sitting down. Disingenuously I explained that I had come to say good-bye, I was going to the farm on Monday.

"Be 'ee, now?" said my Cousin Charles courteously.—I scanned his face for any trace of wistfulness. But as usual he showed no expression at all. He didn't even look impatient—though his next words might have been considered dismissive. "I'll gladly give Clara your kind message," said my Cousin Charles; and after a brief pause added that when her did fare abroad, her was commonly many hours from home.

I refused to take the hint. Instead I asked boldly hadn't he any messages for the farm, because I was sure they all longed for news of him?

He slowly shook his big, handsome head.

"All know I wish 'em well," said he. "There be no news in that."

This was so typically Sylvester, I couldn't argue with it. There was nothing to do but plunge.

"If you were going home too, we could go together," said I, as casually as possible. "Do just think, Charlie, how pleased Aunt Charlotte would be to see you, after all this time! And wouldn't you be pleased too, to see the farm again? And Uncle Tobias and Luke and Matthew, and Aunt Grace and Aunt

Rachel? You can't have *forgotten* them—" here, I must admit,
I finished foolishly—"you can't possibly have forgotten them,
they're too big!"

Foolish as I was, my Cousin Charles looked at me kindly.
For the first time he gave me the good, slow, Sylvester smile.

"Aye," said he, "they'm sizable all right. 'Tis a thing I do
never grow used to, at London: the small stature of the popu-
lation. Do a chap bother Clara, and I be called upon to calm
he, 'tis like taking up a terrier. Or some other small dog."

It was easy to see why my Cousin Charles made such a
splendid chucker-out. He was never afraid of anyone, so he
was never angry. He chucked out a fighting-drunk as he'd have
put out a snapping terrier—quietly, peaceably, without fuss.
(Clara told me he once doused a sparring couple with her washing-up water. One saw how his mind worked: he must have
been regretting they hadn't tails to be picked up by.) But I
wasn't just then concerned with the London career he had so
unexpectedly carved out for himself, and I returned to my main
point.

"You know you want to go home," said I firmly. "And any
way I'm sure it's much better for you to be among people your
own size. I know what it's like myself. The year I had scarlet
fever and had to stay down a class I was top even in mathe-
matics, and it was *extremely* bad for me. Everyone said so."

He looked at me really quite respectfully.—What a picture
we must have presented, I lecturing him from my bentwood
chair, he, three times my weight and size, respectfully inclined!
But again, it was Sylvester: all Sylvesters retaining, no doubt
from the days when they spoke smoothly to Druids, an innate
respect for powers beyond their ken. I could always impress

my aunts with my knowledge of Botany: if I didn't cut the
sacred mistletoe, I could at least draw it. All the same, I felt
I wasn't *influencing* my Cousin Charles. (As probably the
Druids hadn't influenced his forefathers. Send up, when your
turn came round, a white horse for the sacrifice, then go your
way till your turn came round again.) It was without much real
hope of success that I reiterated and elaborated my proposal,
that we should go back to Devon together.

Thoughtfully, kindly, respectfully, my Cousin Charles again
shook his head.

" 'Twouldn't suit," said he.

I felt thoroughly impatient with him. I snapped—like a
London terrier.

"I know a great deal more than you think," said I shortly.
"*I* know Fanny's writing to you, trying to make up your quarrel
with Uncle Tobias; and I think you're very unkind, and very
inconsiderate, and just stubborn like all Sylvesters, not to meet
her halfway."

—When a Sylvester really looked at you, turned on you the
full force of his withdrawn yet contemplative gaze, it was a
test for the boldest spirit. So my Cousin Charles looked at me
now: his eye thoughtful, yet inscrutable; his regard powerful,
yet incalculable. I felt small not only physically. He said calmly,

" 'Ee've the right idea of I 'xactly; and I trust 'ee may pass
a most joyful holiday. And if 'ee looks behind the old pump, 'ee
may find a wren's nest; so small they be, and so bold, as my own
little cousin."

I got myself somehow out of the Saloon. I wished very much
Clara hadn't arranged to stay away so long. *She* might be able
to handle Charles; I certainly was not. I ran back to the Gar-

dens, met Cook—smelling not of trifle but of hair-oil—and plodded crossly home.

3

I WAS still going to the farm. Nothing could prevent that, and certainly my parents had no wish to. My father, I think enjoyed more than anything in his laborious life those two months of absolute solitude in a house large and silent as a pyramid. My mother equally enjoyed her Bournemouth holiday with my brothers; they met Marguerite's family there, and Frederick was encouraged to teach her tennis. I went to Devon as a matter of course. "So healthy for the child!" I heard my mother murmur, over a tea-table, to the mother of Marguerite. "*You*, my dear, bring up a little beauty: *I* must rely on rude health!" I, handing plates, naturally said nothing. But if they only knew, thought I, if they only knew what an extraordinary child I really was— how full of adult business and affairs—they wouldn't dismiss me so lightly. . . .

Monday came at last: Cook took me to Paddington and put me on the train. I was so full of conceited anticipation, I couldn't even bother to wave her, or London, good-bye.

PART FOUR

CHAPTER XVII

I

DURING the first six years of my visiting the farm, I never perceived, between summer and summer, the slightest change there. My uncles, already old to me, did not age: my aunts seemed fixed in a ripe golden maturity. Even the coming of Fanny Davis made immediately no apparent difference; on the contrary, the interest of her arrival, the preparations for her marriage, rather broadened the normal flow of jocund life— my aunts being never so much themselves as with a festivity on hand. Change dated from the last summer only. But change had set in; and though by comparison with what I found *then,* I now found, on the surface, nothing, the deeper change was far more grave.

Everyone was old.

My Aunt Charlotte, at the gate, moved to greet me with a slow, a patient step: her hug was less violent, I had breath, and wits, to *notice:* I noticed at once the streak of grey twining like a ribbon through her plaited crown. Her face, less broad and ruddy, showed the withered-apple look all farm-women put on in time.—But too soon, thought I, too soon! I didn't remark upon it, I had my wits about me; but I scanned my Aunts Grace and Rachel anxiously. They too seemed quite old.—In them the change was less physical, they were younger than Charlotte, Grace's head was still corn-coloured, and Rachel's milky throat still full; but there had come over them both a silence, a settled reserve of manner, too like the indifferent stillness of age. They no longer fripped and quarrelled with each other, but no more had they regained their old good understanding. Their relations had come to a sort of stalemate. Neither Grace nor Charlotte had given way; Fanny Davis still lay entrenched upon her sofa, but Grace no longer admitted her presence. She spoke neither to Fanny nor of her, and refused to set foot in the parlour. In the circumstances no doubt only silence made it possible for my aunts to continue living together at all; it also made them seem very old.

My Uncle Tobias was old absolutely. This I think was due simply to his years, women-matters never much concerning him. Age had come upon him as suddenly as it came upon his father, he left more and more decisions to Matthew, inclined more and more to his father's warm perch by the fire. But Matthew was old too; a little bewildered by his new authority, took advice of Luke and Stephen; who by their equal lack of assurance showed themselves un-young as he. . . . It was in short a moment in the life of the farm like a moment in the life of a tree, when the old leaves are ready to drop, but the new buds do not yet push forth. It was a moment when the Sylvester farm waited a new master.—I had him so to speak up my sleeve —Charlotte's first-born Charles, eldest son of eldest son; for I strongly suspected that no one save myself knew where in the world he was.

Except, of course, Fanny Davis. I make another exception for her: she alone wasn't grown old. *She* looked in fact rather younger than I remembered; her short dark hair now prettily curled, her cheeks, warmed by the parlour fire, prettily pink. A slight new fretfulness in her expression was rather child-like; murmuring, behind Charlotte's broad back, that we must have a long, long talk *soon,* she shot my youth a glance of complicity. I went to bed, that first night, a sadder child than I'd arrived; but as the first days passed, and as I perceived all I have here resumed, I doubt if I grew wiser.

I thought it very lucky I had come, to set all to rights.

Little peace-maker, little match-maker, little know-all that I was, I felt perfectly confident of my ability to do so: it seemed to me simply a matter of giving all my relations a good talking-to. For the one essential was to get Charlie home, after which all would be well again, especially if he married Clara, though even Clara wasn't absolutely necessary; and I knew where Charlie was, and how to summon him. *Tobias* would have to apologise. Whatever their quarrel had been about, and however bitter, Tobias would never, I sagaciously reflected, once it was pointed out to him, allow a point of pride to jeopardise the welfare of the land. So it only needed pointing out to him.

That I did not do so immediately was due to two reasons.

The first was the extreme difficulty of entering into any sort of conversation whatever with my Uncle Tobias. He had never noticed me much, and now did not notice me at all. Even when I planted myself directly before his chair his eye seemed to *omit* me, to pass around me and through me back to the familiar hearth-place; and either my voice was too light to penetrate his deafness, or else he could close his ears, like a hunting dog, against any distracting sound. It wasn't easy work. Much as I longed to present Charlotte with the glorious *fait accompli* (before I gave *her* a talking-to about Clara), I began to fear I should have to enlist her aid first, and thus rather spoil the surprise, with Tobias. . . .

The other reason I delayed was simply that I had so much else to do. I didn't mean to allow myself to be diverted; but it was so intoxicating to have the run of the farm again, to dance in and out looking at new calves, new piglings, new kittens —christening them all with names from Early Roman History —helping or hindering my aunts, eating my head off, sleeping like a kitten myself—cutting the lavender, (a week early), and generally recovering from nine months in London. The weather was superb, all aunts encouraged my fecklessness. —Not of course knowing it to be so; they were encouraging me chiefly, I think, to spend less time in the parlour with Fanny Davis. Charlotte and Grace found me small outdoor tasks and errands, Rachel was always there before me to make Fanny's tea. (Upon Rachel now fell all sick-room duties, which she accepted with nun-like patience, if not with nun-like cheer-fulness.) There was no *time*, during those first bright days, for much well-doing; and I temporarily shelved my responsibilities.

I was so busy, and happy, I didn't even have my long, long talk with Fanny Davis until the Thursday afternoon. My aunts as I say kept me rather from her; and I had also something to decide in my own mind, something that made me not over-anxious for our talk *until* I had decided it, that inclined me against impatience. On the fourth day after my arrival, how-ever, on the Thursday, my Aunt Rachel left Fanny's tea-making to me; possibly because it *was* Thursday, when Miss Jones and Mrs. Brewer came over from Frampton. (They came still. Tuesdays and Thursdays Fanny Davis was still At Home.

THE GIPSY IN THE PARLOUR

My Aunt Rachel no longer gave a penny for her lustre-ware. The first time I saw Rachel indifferently handle a chipped plate, I recognized her old as Charlotte.) At four o'clock I therefore carried up cream and cakes—so Charlotte's Sylvester pride still ordained—and for the first time Fanny Davis and I had the parlour to ourselves.

"As we shall have all evening," said she, with a small, sweet smile. "I've specially warned off both, dear, both the Brewer and the Jones, in order to have at least *one* happy hour quite alone with my little friend. . . ."

CHAPTER XVIII

I

THE fire glowed, the kettle sang; all was as it had been—Fanny snug on her sofa, I snug on the hearth. Once again the old sentimental intimacy enfolded us. "Now tell me all the London news," said Fanny Davis; and then it was I had to make my hitherto postponed decision.

I hadn't told Charlotte I'd seen Charlie. I was still waiting, still hoping for the *fait accompli*. Should I now tell Fanny Davis? I believed her already active on the Sylvester behalf—more active than I'd been, or yet was: Charles's correspondent, urging Charles to wiser courses. Selfishness made me greedy to claim all credit I could; I also, more obscurely, felt it disloyal to Charlotte to give Fanny my news first.—In the event, my tongue made the decision for me.

"Fanny," cried I uncontrollably, "I've seen Cousin Charles!" —And sat back on my heels, not at all sorry to have the words out, feeling extraordinarily important, looking forward to our long, momentous, adult conversation. . . .

"When?" said Fanny Davis.

—She was so much less startled than I expected, I only then realised my thoughtlessness. A slammed door made Fanny tremble; *I* might have made her faint. But though she did quiver, just once, she remained otherwise composed. Her manner in fact became rather business-like; she appeared chiefly —*intent*. She reared and propped herself on one elbow, the better to watch my face. I felt a delicious importance.

"A week ago," said I. "The *last* time. I've been seeing him ever since Christmas."

"Did he come on Christmas Day?"

I was evidently the one who was going to be surprised.

"No, of course not," said I. "He's never been to our house at all.—When I said Christmas, it was really February, only the decorations were still up." (Here of course referring to Jackson's Saloon; it was too complicated to explain, so I let it go. I felt in need of explanations myself.) "Charlie's never come to our house at all," I repeated. "Did you expect him to?"

"It just crossed my mind," said Fanny Davis. "Go on."

"I found him because I took your letter. It was quite close, I thought I might as well. . . . Fanny, when you wrote to him, I mean when you wrote before, did you tell him to come and see us?"

"I may have done," said Fanny carelessly. "In fact, dear, I thought he might well have a word or two with your papa. But he evidently decided otherwise, and you—clever little thing! —found him out for yourself. Go on. Was he very much delighted to see you?"

I hesitated.

"Not exactly *delighted*; at least I don't think so. But you know what Sylvesters are—"

"One can never tell what they're thinking," finished Fanny lightly. "How true that is! Quite possibly he was too touched for speech. But I see he let you into the secret of our correspondence: did he tell you—" here she leant towards me more intently than ever—"did he tell you its subject?"

I said no, but I'd guessed. I said I'd guessed exactly what had happened, Charlie like all Sylvester sons had quarrelled with his father, and they were both so stubborn neither would make up, and Fanny was doing all she could to bring them together again. And I said I thought it perfectly wonderful of her to be exercising from her sickbed such a beautiful influence, and that I was sure all would come right in the end because I was sure Charlie really wanted to come home.—Fanny's lack of answering warmth, as I finished, surprised me. Before my enthusiastic praises she merely dropped back against the cushions, and asked me not to call him Charlie, it was so vulgar.

"It's what Clara always calls him," I apologised. "Fanny, is there anything else Charles could have told me? I mean, have you any *plan*? I tried hard to bring him back myself—"

I broke off. Fanny hadn't moved, or uttered any exclamation; but something made me break off. She was now sitting perfectly still, so rigid indeed that I was filled with alarm, I *had* startled her, I thought, the shock had been but delayed.

"Are you quite well, Fanny?" I enquired anxiously. "Are you sure I'm not tiring you? Wouldn't you sooner rest?"

The breath came out of her body in a long sigh. But she faintly smiled at me.

"Perfectly well, dear," said she. "Go on, go on talking. Who is Clara?"

Still keeping an anxious eye on her, I said Clara was Miss Blow, who managed Jackson's Economical Saloon, where Charlie—Charles—had his lodging. Fanny appeared quite interested, and asked what Clara looked like: I described her at some length, stressing her size and her high colour and the interesting way she did her hair. "Good heavens, dear!" said Fanny lightly. "She sounds exactly like a barmaid!" I had never seen a barmaid, except in *Punch,* but on reflection I saw the justice of Fanny's remark; and a trifle defensively added that Clara was very good-tempered as well. "Poor creatures, they have to be," said Fanny kindly. "Do you know, dear, all you say solves a little mystery that's been troubling *me*. I've assured Charles for months now he may come home and be welcome; no doubt he owes Miss Blow so much for rent, he feels he can't quit without bilking her! Foolish boy!" cried Fanny, quite vivaciously. "Why didn't he apply to Mrs. Toby?—Or to your own papa, dear, really quite a close relation?" (I was quite certain my father wouldn't have advanced Charles a penny, but I didn't say so. I didn't, just then, say anything. I was too much bewildered by this new light on the situation at Jackson's.) "I know what landladies are," continued Fanny feelingly. "I dare say Miss Blow has visited the pawnbroker's already, and poor Charles has no more than he stands up in!—In which case, dear, we must set to work at once; *you* shall tell your tale to Mrs. Toby, and I've no doubt in the world the money will be found. You haven't told her already, I suppose?"

I said no. I was still dreadfully bewildered. Fanny's confident tone, as she so rapidly sketched Charlie's predicament, was wonderfully convincing; at the same time, she didn't *know* Jackson's, she didn't know Clara. I, who did, felt my kind hostess of Brocket Place quite incapable of the behaviour attributed to her. Certainly Charles was in her debt, and possibly for money—unless he'd returned from Australia much richer than his appearance and behaviour suggested; but his chief debt was for kindness. Clara had been very good to him. She had been good *for* him. She could quite easily—I think I now realised this for the first time—have kept Charles in complete idleness, fed by Jackson's plenty; hanger-on instead of chucker-out. Chucking patrons out preserved not only Charlie's physical condition, but also his self-respect; a man's job if ever there was one, chucking-out might well have been Charlie's salvation . . . All these thoughts crossed my mind too rapidly for coherent voicing; but I was left with so strong a conviction that Clara was being misjudged, I felt I had better tell Fanny everything.

"She isn't like that *at all*," said I.

"Who isn't, dear? You can't mean Mrs. Toby!" exclaimed Fanny. "Good heavens, child, to bring her Charles home she'd sell the pianoforte!"

"Of course I don't mean Aunt Charlotte," said I, "I mean Clara. Clara isn't like that at all, I'm sure she'd never pawn Charlie's clothes if he owed her a hundred pounds. She's too fond of him. And I think he's fond of her. Do you know what *I* think, Fanny? I think they're going to get married."

So I thought, so I said, with perhaps rather remarkable confidence. What I *did* was more remarkable still. My wildest dream came true: I cured Fanny Davis.

2

MIRACULOUSLY, she rose. She rose to her feet. She stood. Quite unsupported, Fanny Davis stood. My Aunt Charlotte's Paisley shawl slid unregarded about her feet, the cushions dropped to lie among its folds—so briskly did Fanny rise. With a quick motion she pushed all this encumberment aside, and stood free.

"Fanny!" I gasped—leaping up in my turn to hold her. "Fanny, be careful! Lie down again at once!"

She laughed. Certainly she didn't seem to need my help; I was astonished by the erectness of her back, the thrust of her shoulders, against my protective arm.

"Dear little friend!" smiled Fanny Davis. "Didn't good Dr. Lush always pronounce my ailment nervous? So it was, indeed; now by some magic my nerves are tuned again. You observed, did you not, how I flinched, some moments ago? It was then I felt strength return. . . ."

Most patently strength had returned. After a moment, while I still gaped, Fanny with an experimental air began to pace about the room; pausing indeed now and again to hold by the mantel, or by a chair-back; but every moment with increasing assurance. Life and vigour, as I watched, flowed back into her limbs.—I still couldn't believe it, I still expected to see her suddenly collapse; but round and round the parlour Fanny paced, at the last whisking her skirts like the train of a ball-gown, at last pausing by the piano—but still on her feet—to thrum out a dance-tune.

"I danced to *that* at the Assembly," said Fanny Davis, "and I shall dance to it again!"

It was then I rushed out upon the landing, and hurled myself downstairs, to proclaim to all the household that Fanny was cured.

Up trooped my aunts, marvelling—even Grace, swept along by the general impetus. Fanny Davis received them with every caress, kissing their broad astounded cheeks, dropping upon Rachel in particular tears of gratitude; paced again about the parlour to show her strength. What had cured her, all marvelled? Could it be, said Fanny Davis, smiling, the pleasure of having her own little friend back again? What else could it be? (I conceitedly received my aunts' looks of renewed surprise.) But hadn't good Dr. Lush always proclaimed her ailment nervous? "What matters *how,* you dear good souls, so long as it is?" cried Fanny Davis. . . .

I think I noticed even then, even through the rosy clouds of self-conceit, that she had never so vivaciously addressed them before. Even in her first days of health and strength, Fanny Davis had been humbler. She wasn't now humble at all.—The Bible tells so little of Lazarus' post-mortem behaviour; we had no standard by which to judge Fanny's, raised as she was too, almost, from the dead. *I* found her vivacity at once natural, and disconcerting; I also remembered that as I dashed out and down, calling to my aunts, Fanny sent no call after me for her betrothed.—Stephen, I thought remorsefully, Stephen, surely, should have been first to know?—But Fanny hadn't called upon Stephen, nor had I thought to seek him; and when I now suggested I should do so, Fanny said, no, not just yet.

In fact there descended on the parlour, at my helpful words, a rather odd silence. Kisses and caresses over—my Aunt Grace, under her share of them, still a trifle poker-backed—what was to do was so obviously to find and gladden my Uncle Stephen, that Fanny's withdrawal struck an awkward note. "B'aint 'ee quite sure then of recovery?" enquired my Aunt Charlotte, with a touch of Grace's tone. "Afore all else, us mustn't raise unconscionable hopes in he," said my kind Aunt Rachel; "take two-three days more, Fanny Davis, till all strength be confirmed!" "Be Fanny recovered, Stephen did ought to know instantly," said Grace. "Matrimony being so far out of his mind —this two-three year, Rachel!—Stephen did ought to be apprised of his happy fate without delay."

Erect upon the hearth, but now, it seemed, holding herself so upright with a little more of effort, Fanny looked only at Charlotte.

"Let me talk to Mrs. Toby first," said she.

CHAPTER XIX

I

I SEE now that from Fanny Davis' point of view I had precipitated things. She herself had been impulsive, even rash; had sprung too soon to her feet, too soon let me run to spread the glad news of her recovery. Now she had to make the best bargain she could. *I* had no idea of any bargain to be made at all, I was simply intensely interested; and being not absolutely driven from the parlour, let my Aunts Grace and Rachel quit it without me; saw Fanny by a look admit my presence; and so hovered at the door.

"Dear Mrs. Toby," said Fanny Davis, "what I have to confess is a tale of love . . ."

And out she, suddenly tearful, sobbed it; and as I now resume it—to me no less astonishing than to my Aunt Charlotte—I see it all explicable, and the whole gist of it to be summed, in the phrase that equally sums Fanny's character.

She knew how to seize a chance.

She didn't put it like that herself.

"It was love at first sight, dear Mrs. Toby," wept Fanny Davis. "Between one dance and the next, between one figure and the next, we read *all*, in each other's eyes. The French call it the *coup de foudre*."

171

So that was what had happened, at the Assembly: Fanny Davis and my Cousin Charles fell in love. They looked in each other's eyes and were lost to all—save possibly, on Fanny's part, to the main chance. If so, with what boldness and resolution she seized upon it! She was to marry Stephen in three days. She was at the Assembly as Stephen's bride. Between one dance and the next—between one figure and the next—she not only fell in love, she made up her mind. Did she also, then and there, make up her plan?

She didn't lead us to believe so. She fell sick next day, she assured Charlotte, from pure agony of spirit.

"For consider my position!" begged Fanny Davis. "Not only had I poor Stephen to think for, I had also, a little, *myself*. The misconstructions I might have been open to, changing from younger to elder!—Not in years, of course—poor Stephen! —but so far as concerned all position! To marry Charles, *your* son, would alter my situation completely, from being last I should be first; and weak, even deceitful as it was to keep silent, Charles himself urged it, till health should be restored."

My father was a barrister. I had enough legal blood in me to realise, dimly, that something was being *put* to Charlotte. She hadn't asked why Fanny kept silent; if she did, she was answered in advance.—But of this Charlotte herself probably saw nothing. She hadn't yet spoken. She stood exactly where Grace and Rachel had left her, without stirring, letting Fanny talk; needing perhaps so many reiterations—her silence forcing Fanny into repetition—before she could finally comprehend what she heard.

"So you'm betrothed to my son Charles," said she at last. "Be that it, Fanny Davis?"

I thought Fanny controlled a movement of impatience. But her voice remained smooth as silk.

"Yes, indeed, dear Mrs. Toby," said she. "Can you find it in your heart to blame me? He quite god-like in his handsomeness! The French call it the *coup de foudre.*"

" 'Tis called something other, in Devon," said my Aunt Charlotte. "What of my kind brother Stephen?"

"Stephen," said Fanny firmly, "will *understand.* I shall always have the greatest regard, the kindest sisterly affection for him; for the very reason that he of all men would never wish me to marry against the dictates of my heart. But for my illness, making *any* marriage impossible, Stephen should of course have been told long since!" (Again, I felt that something was being *put.* I also, for the first time, realised, as a criticism, that Fanny talked like a novelette.) But before I had time to examine either reflection, she had hurried on. "I see you wonder," pursued Fanny rapidly, "why Charles ever left my side? *That* I can explain at once. He couldn't endure to see me so weak: the first time he'd loved, his feelings I can only compare to a volcano! He couldn't endure to see me, he couldn't endure not to; and *now,* though I've assured him again and again that his presence would quite restore me—as indeed the mere account of him has, from our little friend—" here Fanny raised a beckoning hand—"what do I learn *now,* from our little friend? That poor Charles is so indebted to his landlady—in other circumstances quite laughable!—he's not able to leave London!"

My Aunt Charlotte bent on me, as I advanced, a heavy, anxious look.

"Be it true, as Fanny says?" asked she.

I said stubbornly, no.

Nothing supported me, at that moment, but my affection for Clara Blow. I liked Clara. I loved her—far better, as I'd never till that moment realised, than I loved Fanny Davis. So I said no. I said Clara Blow, and I was very sorry I hadn't told about her before, was a particular friend of mine; and that she was so good-natured and generous, I was quite sure that whether Charlie'd paid her or not, and I thought in a way he had paid her, she would never try and stop him coming home.

Fanny Davis shot me an ambiguous glance.

"Sweet, innocent child!" said she. "Whom neither you nor I, Mrs. Toby, could wish to disillusion!—Don't be stupid, dear: naturally Miss Blow wants her money—as naturally as Charles can't compound for it.—For if he *wished* to marry her," snapped Fanny Davis, I cannot but think rashly, "what was to stop him?"

My Aunt Charlotte lifted her head.

"Maybe his parents' consent," said she. "Maybe he still have the grace to ask for that . . . Do 'ee like this Clara, my dear?"

I was about to say I liked her very much, when Fanny interrupted.

"As Charles and I ask it now!" she cried. "Dear Mrs. Toby, let me be your daughter! To me at least how natural, how sweet the relationship will seem! How far, far more natural than any other! Let your kind, generous heart have its way, and welcome me in!"

"My kind, generous heart," repeated Charlotte. She appeared to consider the words, to examine them intellectually; I, knowing that heart's long battle with Grace Beer, to save Fanny from being turned away, read at least some part of her mind. To have done good, and see evil come of it, was a paradox that so caught as it were her moral attention, she simply set the rest of Fanny's words aside. Or perhaps they too deeply offended her taste . . .

Fanny Davis, after a moment, shrugged.

"Hard as Pharaoh's, I see!" observed she whimsically. "How fortunate that I can console myself with Charles'! When you're a little recovered, shall we discuss ways and means? To take up the money in person will I think be so much the best; and if a matter of twenty pounds, or forty, or even more—to have Charles home again, won't it be *amply* worth it?"

However veiled, this was a declaration of war. Rebuffed—as she undoubtedly was, no emotional appeal could have fallen flatter—rebuffed, Fanny declared war; and her smile, lifting a narrow lip above teeth so small and sharp, was victorious already. With a pang of dismay I perceived how *sure* she was— sure of Charles, sure of herself. To-day, in fact, I see her pretty emotional appeal as nothing more or less than an exercise in virtuosity. Fanny Davis (again the gloss is to-day's), took a virtuoso's pleasure in pitting her silver tongue against odds. For once it had failed; but it didn't matter, because she was so sure.

"Train-journeys are so remarkably easy," added Fanny Davis, "I dare say I'll have him home before the week's out. . . ."

Setting this aside too, setting all aside, my Aunt Charlotte slowly turned herself towards the door.—I suppose that of all the changes that in the past two years had come over her, this was the greatest: she could no longer be angry. Only a twelve-month ago, at such a tale of treachery, she would have trampled Fanny Davis underfoot—if not quite literally, then at least morally: loosed upon her such a storm of wrath, such a violence of indignation, that Fanny must have been blown about like a leaf in a gale. Now anger failed her. It was as though, in the long battle with Grace Beer, my Aunt Charlotte had fought herself out.

"You tell I more than I can compass," said she heavily. "I must speak wi' my sisters. Can 'ee get yourself to bed, or shall Rachel still assist 'ee?"

"Dear me, no," said Fanny Davis. "Since I may be off to London in *no* time, I must learn to practise my powers!"

Gravely, my Aunt Charlotte nodded, and went out; and I ran after her.

2

"Aunt Charlotte," cried I, on the landing without, "I didn't know! If I'd known, about Fanny and Charles, I'd have told you! I didn't know!"

"No more than any one of we," agreed my Aunt Charlotte soothingly. "Do it seem so mistaken a match to 'ee too?"

I stammered yes, because of Clara. Stammering out more about Clara, and about Charles in London, I grew finally incoherent; my Aunt Charlotte picked me up and carried me to bed. She was still strong enough for that; strong enough for any act of compassion. But she was no longer listening to me very attentively; already her thoughts seemed withdrawn where I could not follow them; by her face, she contemplated catastrophe. I stopped talking and and lay quiet. Whatever had hap-

pened, whatever was going to happen, it was no longer a matter
for children.

3

EMOTION had so worn me out that I fell asleep immediately.
I must have slept a long time, perhaps my full night's stretch:
for when I awoke, or rather when I was awakened, it was to
the unmistakable lack-life, ebb-tide silence of the smallest
hours.

I woke because Fanny Davis was standing by my bed.

She held a candle: its light threw dark shadows under her
eyes; her short dark hair, newly-brushed, haloed her head with
smoke. She was wrapped in Charlotte's Paisley shawl, but no
plum-colour reflected from it on her cheeks, they were white as
wax. White-faced, smoke-haloed, Fanny Davis stood over me;
and this was the first time I felt afraid of her.

"Dear little friend!" said Fanny Davis softly. "Do I startle
you? But wake up, dear; you and I must positively have one
moment's little talk."

I pulled myself up, pressing my shoulders hard against the
bed-head; Fanny Davis sat down at its foot. Her fingers sheltering the candle were so thin, I fancied I could see the bones.

"For you mustn't, you know," continued she softly, "talk quite
so much of poor Miss Blow. It may give a wrong impression.
It may bring Charles trouble. When he and I rule here, naturally you'll be our most welcome little guest; but not if you've
made trouble."

I assured myself I had no reason to be afraid. But I didn't

immediately answer, in case my voice should prove less brave than my spirit. Fanny Davis, watching me, smiled.

"Let me help you, dear," said she gently. "If there's still a struggle in that loyal little breast, let Fanny help. I've no doubt in the world Miss Blow did all she could to win your affection, to insinuate herself into your good graces; but consider with what motive? To enlist you on her side in her ridiculous design to marry Charles. That *he* had no such design is certain—for if he'd wanted to marry her, what prevented him? Certainly not the lack of his mother's consent!" said Fanny Davis, with a little laugh. "It was his engagement to *me*, dear, which he *chose* to keep. Now do you see your foolishness?"

I still couldn't answer her. All she said sounded so sensible, so likely; yet it didn't tally with what I knew of Clara Blow. I still thought that when Clara gave me buns it was out of sheer good-heartedness, not to insinuate herself into my graces. —The implication in any case unflattering. Yet had not Fanny herself, in the course of our first conversation of all—which the present, more momentous one so oddly paralleled in night-shaded secrecy—had not Fanny herself sought my favour with a bag of sweets? Did all adults, in fact, rate all children so low? Did Fanny, in short, know what she was talking about? I had lost confidence in my judgment. I had been so blind, in regard to Fanny and Charles, that my thoughts ran malleable as the wax that slid down Fanny's taper. . . .

If *I* had strayed far in thought, so it seemed had she. As though forgetting that she waited for an answer from me, suddenly, softly, she spoke again.

"The first night I ever spent under this roof," said she softly, "do you know what an odd thing I did?"

I waited. I waited most eagerly.

"I couldn't sleep," pursued Fanny Davis—almost as though speaking to herself. "I got up, and dressed, and went out. By the kitchen-entry, like a servant . . . But I walked all round the house. I remember standing under the crab-tree, in the little court below what was then *your* room, and looking up at the windows. Do you know what I thought, *then?*" asked Fanny Davis, suddenly bending back to me. "As I stood looking up at this great, proud, overbearing house?"

"Yes," said I. "That you wanted it."

She laughed a little.

"For what? There's the real joke.—What I thought, *then*, was but that I at least would never be its servant. As I saw all Sylvester women, even Mrs. Toby. *I* thought it better to be mistress." She paused, her face oddly rapt. "Did my spirit, even then, unaware, reach out to Charles? Perhaps," said Fanny Davis softly, "indeed, perhaps. . . ."

I stirred uncomfortably. With a swift return to lightness, she laughed again.

"And very knowledgeable my spirit was, dear, for mistress I certainly shall be!—*Now* do I see you deciding to be sensible? I think I do. . . . Always my little friend, from the very first days! And my little messenger to Charles as well—which Mrs. Toby, upon reflection, mayn't find quite so endearing as I do. But you shall always find a welcome with *me*: and one of the first things I shall do will be to put you back in your old pretty room."

Without, suddenly, a cock crew.—Just as I was at last about to speak, to protest I was sure my Aunt Charlotte didn't blame me, I was sure she'd keep on inviting me to the farm for ever, a cock crew; and Fanny, always startled by any country-sound, slipped swiftly to her feet, and dipped to my pillow.

"Now sleep, if not beauty-sleep, for both of us!" she cried softly. "Good night, little friend!"—and kissed me, and was gone.

CHAPTER XX

I

In one thing at least, among all my miscomprehensions, I was perfectly right. I wasn't to be blamed. When I joined my aunts at breakfast their looks were kind, exonerating me; and that although, as I saw at once, they *knew*. Charlotte must have talked long, over-night, with Grace and Rachel; they were grave and heavy-eyed, silent and deeply troubled. But I was once more in their confidence, as they were in each other's; the realisation helped me through my bread-and-butter.—As Charlotte cut it for me I saw, for the first time, a clumsiness in her motions: she took up the wrong knife, too blunt, let it slip against the crust and cut her hand; left a smear of blood on the cloth as she pushed the board across to Grace, who silently received it. The year before, Rachel at least would have been loud in sympathy, the day before, Grace bitter in mockery; now neither uttered a word. My uncles apparently noticed nothing; perhaps they had grown used to their wives' silence; the quality of their own was unchanged. *They* didn't know. If it was not a matter for children, no more, I soon understood, was it a matter for men.

It was a matter for the Sylvester women.

THE GIPSY IN THE PARLOUR

As soon as the males had tramped out my Aunt Grace warned me against any rash speech, in especial to Tobias.

"Charlotte being fearful," said she plainly, "lest he do Charles an injury. If there be one crime Sylvesters do hate and despise above all others, 'tis deceitfulness; and Charlie have deceived all two mortal years. 'Ee won't remember, my dear, though maybe Rachel do, time Matthew entered into secret negotiation wi' they Pomfrets as to selling our ten-acre field: they making so brave an offer for it. Tobias laid he out wi' one blow upon the moment of revelation. And as to poor Stephen, 'twould so horribly shock he, till all be most fixed and certain best say no upheaving word. Charlotte, bind up that wound."

It was strange to hear Grace take the lead; but Charlotte sat withdrawn in thought—silent, passive, will-less, seemingly, as her father-in-law at the last, in that very chair, had sat before her. Her hand still bled a little; from time to time she looked at it, pressed it against her apron, and let it lie. The look I had glimpsed on her face the night before, a look, most new to her, of withdrawal, seemed already the settled cast of her countenance; the new lines already engraved. Grace by taking up the burden of leadership did Charlotte kindness; as my Aunt Rachel, in her degree, poured Charlotte a last extra cup.—It was my only consolation, to see them thus re-united, no longer at odds, at last come together again. My own readmittance to their confidence I felt almost undeserved; but as we sat about the breakfast-table—the men gone out, Fanny furnished by Rachel with a tray—I felt myself for the first time, as we talked together so gravely, truly one of the Sylvester women. . . .

"'Tis so hard to credit," sighed my Aunt Rachel, "I credit

it scarcely yet. Have Fanny also deceived we two mortal years?"

"And would two years more," said my Aunt Grace.

"It was what the French call the *coup de foudre*," I put in. "I think that means it's like a thunderbolt. I mean, when Fanny and Charles fell in love, at the Assembly."

"No doubt but Charlie'd turn any head living," agreed Rachel unhappily. " 'Ee didn't see he, my lamb; but for dancing, and deportment, and brave Sylvester looks, him outshone all. . . . What remains mysterious to I be how *her* so turned his?"

"Didn't Charlotte say herself, on Fanny's first coming, her charm be felt by males solely?"—This was my Aunt Grace; speaking however without the least malice; speaking rather as a doctor of a disease. "Moreover, Fanny in her peacock gown were no poor sight. . . ."

"Which Charlotte purchased for she her own self," sighed Rachel—again, unmaliciously; *diagnosing*. "I do believe maybe that compassed it, Grace; for I saw Luke's eye also on her bosom; so cunningly displayed it were, the blue showing off its milk-whiteness, I saw Luke's eye stray also. 'Tis certain Fanny have a charm for males."

"Question be," said Grace sharply, "how far 'twill overbear all else. Can her put Charles so at loggerheads with all Sylvesters, to wed without his parents' blessing? Which Charlotte at least I be sure will never give?"

But no promptings roused Charlotte. She might not have heard a word we said. She had—withdrawn.

"Dear soul!—and what of Stephen?" cried Rachel—even her mild tones almost impatient. "How'm Stephen to fare here, how'm he to bide here even, seeing his own betrothed Charlie's bride?"

"Seeing she walk nightly to Charlie's bed," said my Aunt Grace crudely. "Think of that, will 'ee? No male flesh and blood's to endure it—even so sainted a flesh as Stephen's may now appear. 'Twill drive he from home. First of all Sylvesters, him'll be driven from his home."

"I think also of the young ones," said Rachel. "Charlotte did once proclaim Fanny a likely breeder: after her two years' sickness, can us think so still? But to fall in love, seemingly, strikes she down; I say that to carry a nine-months babe be utterly beyond her powers. And 'tis now more than ever before the farm do need a new, strong generation."

"Would 'ee call home your own two from Canada?"

"My two be faring so bravely." (I must repeat it, not one of these exchanges carried a hint of malice. My Aunt Rachel stated a fact: *her* two were faring so bravely, they'd sent her at Christmas such a beaver muff as Frampton never saw.) "So stoutly they'm making their way, to recall they would be a most wrong act," said my Aunt Rachel, almost sorrowfully. "It must rejoice we to know the same of yours—and of Charlotte's second also. Charlie be here at hand, returned as though by Providence."

"Not if he'm to wed Fanny Davis," said Grace.

So we talked, in grave unhappy tones, my Aunts Grace and Rachel and myself, round the remainder-cluttered breakfast-table, my Aunt Charlotte still saying nothing; until presently, as from all our talk no more emerged than the catastrophe's completeness—diagnosis, not remedy—we too fell silent. Grace could take the lead only so far; my Aunt Rachel follow only in lamentation. So we fell silent.

—And so, incredibly, heard the parlour-clock strike. It hadn't struck for two years, its chimes stopped to spare Fanny's nerves. It was a piece of sheer impishness on her part, to pause and set them off again, on her way downstairs.

2

SHE entered with a light and sprightly step: cool and trim, her short hair neatly combed over her forehead, her dress, mysteriously less limp, freshened by a little white lace collar.—There was nothing grand in all this, it was no more than any clever woman could have done for herself. The effect produced was disproportionate. As my aunts, three big, aproned women, rose instinctively to their feet, Fanny might have been the mistress of the house visiting her kitchen.

"Good morning," said she, smiling. "You see I practise my powers. . . . I suppose they all know, Charlotte?"

This was the first time, I noticed it, she ever called my Aunt Charlotte anything but Mrs. Toby. If Charlotte noticed too, she gave no sign.

"All know," she agreed. "Us have just been discussing 'ee; 'ee and Charlie." She turned back to the table, and from it carried a pile of plates to the washing-up bowl. The china clinked as she moved; and Fanny Davis, looking after her, smiled again.

"And what all know, all don't quite like?" she suggested lightly. "In time no doubt I shall have gratitude, for bringing Charles home again!" She sat down: all my aunts being on their feet, this gave her more than ever the air of the mistress; in kind, explanatory tones, she continued. "For it's quite obvious things can't go on here as they are," said Fanny Davis. "But for my illness, I must have acted *long* since!—you good creatures growing more toil-worn every day, and the farm on its rapid way to ruin!"

Across the stillness, for no one immediately spoke, anger rippled like a catspaw over water. I saw my Aunt Rachel lift up her head incredulously, the colour flame in Grace's cheek; while Fanny sat and smiled.

Grace found speech first.

"Leaving we for the moment aside," said she, "and what do '*ee* know of the farm, may I ask?"

"Only what all Frampton knows," said Fanny Davis carelessly—but with what deadly aim! "As to general mismanagement, you know, and bad judgment, and all that. As to Luke and Matthew spending *rather* much time in the George, on market-day; Tobias such a sad lack! I'm told old Mr. Sylvester went quite the same way," sighed Fanny Davis, "but *he*, of course, could lean on Tobias. . . ."

This no one answered. There was no answer. What Fanny had gleaned from her gossips was no more than my aunts must long have known, though without ever openly admitting it; even I had perceived the life of the farm as it were slowing down, losing momentum. Fanny Davis couldn't be answered because she spoke the truth—and not least as to my aunts themselves. They did now seem toil-worn, old and patient and toil-worn, slow-moving and silent, with no more laughter in them . . . But only since Fanny came!—I nearly cried this revelation aloud, as I suddenly perceived the whole sequence of events since she first set foot in my aunts' parlour. That I had been most beguiled of all made my disillusion but completer. "Only since *she* came!" I wanted to cry; but what was the use? She had come. She sat amongst us now, small, trim and composed, fronting the three big Sylvester women with utter assurance; smiling at them.

"So you see why you owe me gratitude," said she. "For if Charles doesn't soon return to take command, I for one can't conceive what's to become of you all.—Dear me, you'd need a whole almshouse!" cried Fanny gaily. "It might be called the Sylvester Arms!"

It was a dangerous moment, while she laughed. But it passed. Grace had moved only one angry step when a sound from Charlotte halted her. Charlotte had but broken a cup, she did not speak; still, the momentary check gave Fanny time to skim prettily, safely on.

"But Charles *shall* return," she assured them, "and for your part you mustn't, you really mustn't think too hardly of me. Hearts, alas, can't be controlled!"

"Nor appetite?" said my Aunt Grace—a little danger still in her voice. "Nor appetite, Fanny Davis? I b'aint speaking of the lusts of the flesh, Fanny Davis; but of the lust, or appetite, for mastery; which I in my time have striven with, to its casting out. . . ."

Fanny's response to this last challenge was unhesitating. With a most smooth, engaging motion she rose and dipped over upon Charlotte.

"Be cross as you like!" she cried vivaciously. "*This* is where *I* find understanding, in my good Charlotte!" Charlotte stood passive, merely knocking the handle off a cup. "See even the lightest task too much for her!" cried Fanny Davis compassionately. "The first thing *I* shall do, as mistress here, will be to hire some young local girl to relieve her at the sink. For shame, Charlotte!" fluted Fanny Davis. "If I've no servant for you yet, at least let Grace or Rachel take her turn!"

—I still, to-day, cannot believe my Aunt Charlotte capable of deliberate false-dealing; yet while she stood there so humbly, fumbling about her humble task, she had undoubtedly disguised from us all her true formidableness. *My* heart was torn for her; Grace and Rachel watched her anxiously. What we had all forgotten was the Sylvester inability to do two things at once. (Yet how often had I remarked on it, in my uncles!) Charlotte, now Sylvester to the marrow, had been thinking. She had been thinking steadily, as we were soon to discover, for the last hour. The bread-knife slipped because she was thinking, not of bread; thinking of something else, she let even her blood flow unstanched. . . . I do not know who was the more startled, ourselves or Fanny Davis, when Charlotte, most placidly cracking a last plate clean across, finally ceased to think, and presented the result of her thought.

"Grace and Rachel will take their turn sure enough," said she, "while I be at London."

CHAPTER XXI

I

It is extraordinarily difficult to convey, so long after, and now
that running up to London has become in all parts of England
no more than an excursion-commonplace, the impact of my
Aunt Charlotte's placid reply. (The impact all the greater for
the placidity.) To-day, Mothers' Unions, Women's Institutes,
members of the Women's Voluntary Service, descend on London in amiable hordes: conveyed by chartered coaches to in-
spect royal wedding-gifts, applaud local choirs, or just for the
ride. Individual women resort thither no less freely, to meet
friends or fight a sale. Native Londoners, if not of absolutely
sinister appearance, can hardly cross Whitehall without di-
recting some pleasant countrywoman to the Army and Navy
Stores. But at the time of which I write, to visit London was
a considerable undertaking—and this though the train-services
were already excellent. The adventure was rather moral. To
simpler, remoter communities, (amongst which ours about
Frampton must be counted), London and Babylon still called
cousins. Even setting foot to platform at Paddington, our own
West Country terminus, one forded a dubious stream. At the
Great Exhibition of 1851, (the last occasion of any widespread
venturing), several well-known local personalities had their

189

pockets picked. One went to London to a death-bed—if one had a relative so misguided as to die there—or, if one was a more than usually important farmer, to the Fat Stock Show. That *I* travelled regularly back and forth was a local wonder, productive of prestige to the Sylvesters, an exaggerated estimate of my parents' income, and equally exaggerated prophecies of my own early demise. . . .

Thus to hear Charlotte speak so placidly of going to London naturally astounded us all. Fanny Davis recovered her wits first.

"To London!" cried she. "You go to London? Dear Charlotte, but why?"

"To have a word wi' my son Charlie," returned Charlotte calmly. Still calmly—how we had under-estimated her!—she surveyed the china-wreckage about the sink, and with a casual gesture intimated that Rachel might put all away. "Naturally save what be damaged," said she, with a lightness to rival Fanny's. "That throw out, bor; Sylvesters b'aint used to mended crockery. . . . Yes, b'aint it true," said my Aunt Charlotte, "only thought brings wisdom how to act? So my thoughts be come to their issue: all 'ee tells of you and he do still seem so astounding, and so full of import moreover to all of we, and so unvouched for moreover by Charlie's own self, I've a mind to seek he out in London, if but to set my own thoughts at rest."

"Charlotte!" breathed my Aunt Rachel. "Oh, Charlotte, b'aint 'ee the masterpiece!—and 'ee shall have my beaver muff."

IT took five days to get my Aunt Charlotte and Fanny off to London.—For Fanny went too. Upon this she was absolutely determined, her pretext being to take care of Charlotte on the journey; and though all strongly suspected the more interested motive of aiming to stiffen Charlie's neck, there were reasons why no one attempted to stop her. Charlotte was by no means averse from company, even in her heyday a trip to London would have seemed a very venturesome act, and from a practical point of view Fanny was obviously best spared at the farm. (I spent all my eloquence begging Charlotte to take *me*—pressing my claims as native Londoner, seasoned train-catcher, friend of Clara Blow. To no avail. It was not a matter for children.) In addition my Aunts Grace and Rachel wanted to turn out the parlour, which they could do far best in Fanny's absence. They were so in love with this project I believe they would actually have *pressed* Fanny's going, had she needed it; oblivious of the situation's irony. For quite possibly they would be readying the same chamber to receive again, after two years, a same bride, but different groom. . . .

It took five days to get Charlotte and Fanny off, because there was so much to prepare.

In the first place, they took their food.

Neither I believe contemplated a stay of more than two or three nights at most. They still took food. All knew there was food to be had, in London; I myself, for example, somehow subsisted through each winter; still, they took provisions.

We baked. Large pasties, in form borrowed from our Cornish neighbours, we acknowledged the most nourishing food portable. We therefore baked pasties. My Aunt Charlotte, I think with some idea of bearing gifts, ordained cakes also: the kitchen smelled like Christmas. There was also the matter of breakfast; so they took eggs, and a tea-caddy.

There was, also, the matter of their costumes. My Aunt Charlotte's wardrobe was perfectly adequate to her station, and Rachel lent her beaver muff; certain froggings of black braid were nonetheless transferred from a mantle of Grace's to Charlotte's Sunday-best; the whole presenting a rather military, hussar-like effect, on Charlotte's tall figure undeniably impressive. All the flowers were cut from her best bonnet, steamed, and re-attached; the strings were treated similarly, also ironed. Her skirt and bodice were sponged with vinegar. Her underlinen required no attention at all, the store was so great and so immaculate we had but to pick out the best: two of each, and one dozen cambric handkerchieves, still bearing her maiden-cypher. . . .

My aunts were wonderfully fair-minded women. Thoroughly as they now disliked and distrusted her, everything that could be done was done for Fanny also.—Or was this but one more manifestation of the Sylvester pride? Looking back, I think it may have been; I cannot recall anything they did for Fanny with their own hands, as they so eagerly laboured for Charlotte. What I do recall is the point of irony in Grace's voice as she remarked—Fanny possessing no mantle at all, only a shawl—'twas pity Charlotte spent all on a ball-gown. . . . They allowed her, however, full turn at the ironing-board, and the use of a kettle to steam her black straw hat—only it was too far gone to respond—and the use of their work-baskets; which Fanny, with a small smile, accepted. She withdrew, during these days, a great deal of her pretensions: *I* thought biding her time. So far as millinery went, she could have none: it appeared that the contents of her carpet-bag had never been augmented by so much as a shift from the first-class dressmaker in Plymouth. Fanny possessed the dress she stood up in, and two limp dresses more, and a peacock silk ball-gown. *Her* underlinen all charitably agreed to ignore.

My Aunt Charlotte, in all this bustle, was rejuvenated.

I can see now that bustle, during the last two years, had been precisely what she lacked: quietude was more than unnatural, it was unwholesome to her. The bare effort of keeping her voice down, so as not to upset Fanny's nerves, had worked seriously upon Charlotte's: the necessity of avoiding all house-work-noise made her natural avocation a burden almost unendurable. Like Clara Blow, Charlotte needed to bang about; but let bang could throw off two women's work with one hand, and play 'Chopsticks' with me after supper. Undoubtedly, over the past two years, all female within-door work had been properly done; but unless they made their usual noise about it, unless their own particular racket accompanied their labours, all three of my aunts were left, at the day's end, with too much unexpended energy . . . Now, cooking for the journey, dressmaking till all hours, re-trimming bonnets and sorting linen —vociferous again from one end of the house to the other, because if Fanny was on her feet why should she be treated as an invalid?—my aunts released a two-years' accumulation of noise. To Charlotte, it was like water to a plant. In five days, she looked five years younger.

Fanny Davis, with her small smile, observed and said nothing. I alone, I think, observed *her*. Our relations had cooled; she felt me under her thumb again, but so to speak on my promotion. I was no longer so unquestionedly her little friend: she suspected me still of a weakness for Clara Blow.—Which indeed I still harboured, to my unhappiness; for I alone—again —saw Fanny likelier than Charlotte to win the battle in London.

Because I knew Fanny Davis so well. The scales of romantic attachment dropped from my eyes as completely as suddenly: children so hate duplicity. I couldn't forgive her two-years' foxing of me, her joining with me in surmise as to my Cousin Charles' whereabouts—as she had done, more than once, probably with a letter from him in her pocket. I nonetheless admitted her cleverness—because she *had* foxed me. Upon perfectly dispassionate reflection, I rated her so much cleverer than my Cousin Charles, or my Aunt Charlotte, or Clara Blow, I didn't see how one of them, or all combined, stood a chance against her.

Moreover, if Charlotte looked rejuvenated, Fanny Davis looked pretty.

Bustle, astonishingly enough, appeared to suit her also. Dipping between work-basket and kettle—all her movements informed by what I can only describe as *irony*—Fanny Davis also, quietly, bloomed. She found a way of arranging her short hair that was almost fashionable: an Alexandra fringe kissed her eyebrows. I thought of Clara's galumphing coiffure, and hoped Charles insensible to elegance. Hoped, but unconvincedly; all male Sylvesters having a curious knack of seizing upon the currently admired. . . .

There arose also, discussed against the smell of baking and

hot irons, the question of where Fanny and Charlotte should lodge.

Here Charlotte spoke strongly: all reputable Norfolk having from time immemorial put up at the Flower in Hand, by Bishopsgate Station. My Aunt Grace proposed the Bush, time immemorial used by Devon folk, hard by Paddington; so that one felt as 'twere the West Country *backing* one, by its regular service of powerful trains.—Most quietly, now, most insinuatingly, Fanny Davis put in her words; weren't both these nice places, however nice, really no more nor less than *public houses?* For two females alone perhaps—unsuitable? "A small, quiet hotel," suggested Fanny Davis, "if one can't stay with one's friends, or relations—wouldn't some small, quiet hotel be *really* more suitable?"

I felt her eye on me as she spoke. She had already breathed to me a plan which I at once saw impossible, of staying with my parents. I said firmly that I knew of several small, quiet hotels. Fortunately no one took any notice of me; pressed, I could have named only Claridge's.

"Where Fanny bides I naturally mayn't control," said Charlotte more firmly still. "Where I bide will be the Flower in Hand."

Of course Fanny had no choice, because Charlotte would be paying. They went to the Flower in Hand.

3

I can no better describe the scope of these preparations than by saying that my uncles noticed them; with the consequence that Charlotte was forced into the first untruth I ever heard her tell.

She said she was taking Fanny to London to see a doctor.

It was either tell that, my aunts agreed amongst themselves, or tell all, and Fanny Davis acquiesced in the deception. She was I think no more eager than they to thrust enlightenment upon Stephen any sooner than necessary; for all her confidence in his understanding—which she never ceased to affirm—she could not fail to anticipate a painful moment. "Only that, dear, no more," she assured me more than once. "That it must be painful, to both of us, goes without saying; but as soon as the first shock is over, Stephen will understand. Indeed, I some-times think he has forgotten me already!—during this last year almost ceasing to visit my couch! Still, it will be better all the same to have Charles at my side—such a weak little person as I am! Don't imagine for one moment, dear, I accuse my poor Stephen of *fickleness*: it's just that I know he'll regard it as a happy release . . ."

Fanny therefore practised her powers only when the men were abroad; retreating, at their return, from the ironing-board in the kitchen to the parlour-couch; and only occasion-ally, to demonstrate the improvement on which Charlotte based her great plan, making a sort of official appearance on the landing.—The first time my Uncle Stephen saw her there I happened to be present; and as he slowly, almost timidly mounted towards her—Fanny at last on her feet again, though at this moment a little drooping—I felt the pain already on us. My Uncle Stephen's face was so set in lines of patience, he could hardly achieve a smile; but his patient voice lifted.

"Be 'ee truly better, Fanny, my dear?" said he. "Be 'ee truly on the way to recovery?"

Fanny Davis drooped a little more.

"Who knows?" she murmured. "Oh, Stephen, who can tell? Pray, pray don't build your hopes!"

He reached her side and cautiously took her hand. Fanny allowed it to rest passive on his enormous palm.

"I was never a chap hopeful beyond measure," said he. "But if this London doctor be all Charlotte hears of he, and seeing 'ee already so strengthened of your own nature, give I leave to hope proportionately. Take every care upon the journey, my dear, and confide all troublesomeness to Charlotte."

I learnt, long afterwards, that he sought out Charlotte that same night and pressed upon her his personal fortune of twenty pounds as fee and journey-money. Charlotte took it. Money was short all round, just then, at the farm, and she had contemplated selling the pair to her tallboy. So she took Stephen's savings because it was the practical thing to do.

My other uncles, as usual, afforded us no clue to their sentiments. Tobias, upon the prospect of his wife's absence for a period of several days, became silent absolutely. ("Charlotte'll win his consent a-bed," said my Aunt Grace—practically.) At least no obstacle was placed in our travellers' path: the baking and dressmaking proceeded in full vigour, I drew several maps, the last shaded, indicating the locality of Brocket Place, five days passed and all was ready.

My Uncle Stephen drove them to the station in our trap. My Aunts Grace and Rachel, and of course myself, trooped out to see Charlotte and Fanny climb up. I remember, crossing the bitterness of being left behind, a sensation of extreme pride in my Aunt Charlotte's splendid, hussar-like appearance. The flowers in her bonnet garlanded her like a victorious warrior; stacked about with baskets of food, as it might have been with the spoils of war, she sat perfectly erect, perfectly composed, perfectly, (to all outward seeming), confident. Beside her Fanny Davis huddled in her shawl, all features extinguished under the limp, drooping brim of her black straw hat. I, and I think I only, caught her glance as the vehicle was set in motion: from under that limp black brim she shot me a look as full of triumph, as of malice.

We who were left behind could now do no more than wait.

CHAPTER XXII

I

WHILE we waited, an odd thing happened. There sprung up at the farm a spirit of gaiety. All our official looks were sober, we never ceased, at least to begin with, to cast most anxious thoughts after Charlotte; thrusting up from which, as snow-drops from hardest winter-soil, gaiety nonetheless peered. My Aunts Grace and Rachel, passing each other in hall or passage-way, exchanged involuntary smiles. Their new-old shouting matches grew gradually hilarious, they began to laugh at any-thing, at nothing, simply to catch up, as it were, on laughter. Rachel, with no need to bake at all, frivolously made dough to cut me a family of cat and kittens: Grace, from the breast-bone of a goose, made me a jumping frog. Also, of course, they turned out the parlour.

I find it hard to discover a comparison for the zeal with which my aunts set about this work. (Or perhaps the mother of a child stolen by gipsies, her offspring regained, might so set about cleansing its body, burning its rags, clothing it afresh.) Every single portable object was carried out onto the landing, and thence, as space became congested, into Fanny's bedroom. The vacant floor was then swept, then polished; the Turkey carpet, hung over a line in the court, beaten into insensibility.

We washed each lustre separately. We rubbed the fire-irons till they shone like gold. Grace took the cabinet-doors off their hinges, the better to scour their panes. Every item of Rachel's lustre-ware was washed in Castile-soap shavings and warm water, before being set back in place. I won delighted praise for my notion of re-stringing the harp, to make it look more seemly, with lengths of discarded fishing-twine. Fanny's sofa was beaten, and polished. The needlework-chair was brushed with two sets of clean brushes—one hard, one soft. We didn't move out the piano, but we polished that too; and I distinctly remember employing my tooth-powder on its keys.

When all was finished, and set back in place, my aunts decided that the carpet should have been *washed*; so took it up again, and while they were about it gave the floor a second beeswaxing, for good measure, and out of sheer light-heartedness.

Even amongst the men I recall, if not gaiety, at least a certain relaxation. Our mealtimes were no less silent, but an over-flow of cake and pastry loaded the table, and my uncles were cheered by nothing so much as food. They ate even more than usual, it may be their contentment had no other spring; but for whatever reason, whether from appetites ideally satisfied, or because they too felt Fanny's absence a relief, the clouds about their heads perceptibly lifted.—The reason for Stephen's lightening of spirit of course needed no conjecture; and shadowed *my* days.

I felt he should be prepared.

This notion, carried from my Aunt Grace scouring the china-cabinet to my Aunt Rachel washing lustre-ware, received small encouragement. Since all things must take their course, said

Grace, and Rachel echoed her, no use to meet trouble halfway —a retreat from reality which shocked me deeply. I forgot that no Sylvester could do two things at once: they couldn't think about Stephen, because their minds were fixed on their parlour. They said Charlotte had bade all keep still tongues. When I persisted that Charlotte had said nothing against Stephen's being prepared, only against his being *told,* they didn't, I think, even hear me. I therefore loitered down to the pig-styes, at the appropriate hour, on a private mission.

My Uncle Stephen was still far easier to draw into conversation than Tobias: he noticed me almost at once, and to my opening remark, that I hoped Charlotte and Fanny got to London safely, replied after only a moment or two, most like they had.

(I should say that I alone, during these few momentous days, watched for a letter. No Sylvester did. I had begged Charlotte to write, or even *telegraph* to us; she nodded the proposal aside as a childish fancy. Even shyer of a pen than most Sylvesters —shy as of some black art—she had neither written to Charlie to meet her, nor allowed me to do so on her behalf. I still hoped for a line from Fanny; which didn't come.)

"How did they *look,* Uncle Stephen?" I asked cautiously. "How did Aunt Charlotte and Fanny seem, when they got to the station?"

He considered. I saw him withdraw his thoughts from me, from the present, and cast them back towards Exeter station. It naturally took a little time.

"Charlotte," said my Uncle Stephen at last, "commanded a chap to bear in their belongings just as 'twere her natural right. . . . As to Fanny, her appeared most amazingly upheld.

Also hopeful," added my Uncle Stephen, after a moment's further research. "In fact, I b'aint able to remember she, my little dear, so uplifted, and so hopeful-seeming, since our first Plymouth meeting . . ."

I was twelve, he nearing forty. I trembled for him. I said impetuously,

"Uncle Stephen, if you don't marry Fanny *ever*, will it wreck your life?"

Like one of our huge farm-horses, like the very incarnation of all docile strength, my Uncle Stephen bent his big head.

"B'aint us all as grass?" said he gravely. "As weeds to be cut down and put in the Lord's oven? Do Fanny grow brave enough to wed, most gladly will I wed she; do her still decline, b'aint I in the happy situation to offer she for ever a kindly home? Where be the wreckage of my life in that?"

He spoke poetry, he spoke like the Bible; I nonetheless felt slightly impatient with him. I wished him more, at that moment, the legendary black Sylvester male. I didn't put my last question —what if Fanny, recovered, married anyone else?—I felt so sure he would have a fresh New Testament answer for me. Sylvesters weren't New Testament, they were Old: Tobias, I was certain, would never so tamely have acquiesced in the rape of his bride. (The point wasn't, I in justice repeat, put to Stephen directly; I still, I think accurately, perceived the trend of his mind. My Uncle Stephen was already one step removed from human failings, or feelings. He was Christian. From a worldly standpoint, from the farm's standpoint, a smack of pagan self-regarding would have been more useful.) I said,

"Uncle Stephen, if Fanny gets better, do you mind what she does at all?"

"Not so be it suits she," said my Uncle Stephen, gently.

At least I had prepared him. If the hope that sprung up in my mind, actually during our conversation—the hope that Stephen might by some violent act of will prevent Fanny and Charles from marrying—if this hope was dashed as soon as formed, at least I had prepared him. It seemed unlikely that he would be forced to leave home. But when I said something of the sort to my Aunt Grace, she absently retorted—and only absence could have made her speak so, to me—that 'twould be a very different case altogether, did Stephen ever see Charles and Fanny bedded. I could only hope her mistaken.

2

Two days passed. Three days passed: my Aunt Rachel at least began to wonder had our travellers borne sufficient provision. I confident in the hospitality of Jackson's Economical Saloon, grimly suggested the greater danger of their being run over by omnibuses—because they wouldn't take me with them. Both my aunts regarded this as a joke.—Their laughter rang now continuously as of old, as in the days when I first knew them: each hour of this period carrying so great a respite. Their spirits soared. The parlour, reaching its former pitch of perfection, made their increasing joy. My uncles, stuffed with rich food, yawned contentedly. Lolled in a sunny doldrums, thoughtlessly the Sylvesters took their ease . . .

I was almost lulled into ease myself when on the fourth day Miss Jones called.

It wasn't her usual day. She called as a regular thing, with Mrs. Brewer, because Mrs. Brewer had a pony-cart, on Tuesdays and Thursdays. It may be remembered that it was on a Thursday that I cured Fanny Davis: she and Charlotte left for London the Tuesday following, in which bustle we quite failed to notice the non-appearance of Jones and Brewer. They were sulking because Fanny put them off the Thursday before. (What they missed! For months all Frampton exclaimed it—what they missed!) By the next Thursday, their next regular calling-day, all Frampton knew Fanny and Charlotte set out for London: my Aunt Charlotte's appearance on Exeter station having been relayed back to a Frampton-dwelling cousin by the porter she so majestically commanded there. The presence of Fanny, to him but incidental, naturally whetted local inquisitiveness extremely. In a moment of social honesty, Miss Jones and Mrs. Brewer refrained from calling on that day either. But by the Friday Miss Jones' curiosity got the better of her; and feigning complete ignorance, and a cold in the head to excuse Thursday, on Friday up she drove, lifted by Mr. Simnel the chemist, Taunton-bound.

I was pleased to hear my Aunt Grace dismiss her instantaneously. After in the fewest possible words supplying the least possible information, my Aunt Grace strongly advised Miss Jones to stay by the gate and get a lift back. The Frampton butcher, said my Aunt Grace, should drive past in no more than ten-twenty minutes; and if Miss Jones overlooked a carcase or two from Beer's, there'd easily be room for she. Miss Jones was left at the gate, Grace returned withindoors, myself at her heels. Unluckily, Miss Jones had seen me; and calling out, wouldn't Fanny's little friend bear her company, put me in the helpless position of an elder-summoned child. I halted instinctively; my Aunt Grace, sailing on, left me defenseless. When an elder calls, a child's feet instinctively obey. I turned back to the gate—with what I hoped was a rather cool, ironic look. I nonetheless turned back.

I was at this time continually learning things I didn't want to know.

"So Fanny and Mrs. Toby are gone to London?" said Miss Jones sharply—fixing me with her sharp, blackberry eye. "*That's* a new departure!—Dear me, have I made a pun?"

I elaborately refrained from smiling. I said sulkily, yes, Fanny and my Aunt Charlotte were in Town. I said 'Town,' instead of 'London' to point my own metropolitan superiority. The hit was apparently lost: Miss Jones' blackberry glance looked farther.

"Not, I hope, to consult lawyers?" said she swiftly. "Such ingratitude it would be to Mr. Pascoe! *Have* they, do you think?"

This speech simply baffled me. I knew who Mr. Pascoe was, of course, he was the Frampton attorney my uncles threw out when he approached them after old Mr. Sylvester's death: but why he should be owed gratitude, or what place he could have in our affairs at all, was beyond my comprehension. I maintained however a sulky silence. Miss Jones—and memory dimly recalls some rumour of some attachment, some projected Pascoe-Jones alliance—looked at me impatiently.

"Don't answer if you don't want to," said she. "Such a cross little thing as you are!—Though I may tell you *I* know all about Fanny and Mr. Charles too; and have done these eighteen months; and have a pretty shrewd idea why she and Mrs. Toby are gone to London. *There* I think Fanny quite right; it certainly isn't a wedding for Frampton St. Paul's! But I trust she doesn't set off among the lawyers; and when you write to her, if you won't give *me* her address, you might just remind our dear Fanny that in anything regarding *custom,* a local man is always best."

I should have done better to continue silent. I felt knowledge I didn't want, knowledge I would be happier without, dangerously close. (Not of Miss Jones' complicity; that I had guessed long since, ever since I realised her post-mistress between Fanny and Charles.) Unluckily, the desire to score off her was too strong to be resisted, and I said smartly,

"Customs are something you go through when you come back from France. I don't see that has anything to do with Fanny, or Aunt Charlotte."

Miss Jones laughed.—It was curious; she had picked up, almost exactly, Fanny Davis' laugh. It didn't ripple quite so sweetly, but it was a recognizable echo.

"Indeed no, dear child," rippled—a trifle shrilly—Miss Jones. "I speak of another kind of custom altogether. *Entail*-by-custom, in fact; which if Charles don't establish he may find himself fixed here as hind for ever and a day! They won't be able to sell, my dear, when Tobias pops off; and how will Fanny like that? No London-lawyer can possibly handle it; only a person like Mr. Pascoe, who's seen Sylvesters inherit eldest after eldest just like peers of the realm, has any possible chance of establishing Charles's claim. Write *that* to Fanny Davis, my dear, and I'm sure she'll thank you!"

I stood dumb. Enlightenment—light complex, broken and

refracted, like the light struck from our parlour prisms—enlightenment, however broken, struck me. Half-a-dozen scraps of Fanny's talk dropped together and made sense. I saw how Charles, pleading entail-by-custom, might hope to take the farm absolutely.—Only hope to: lawyer's child that I was, used all my life to overhearing legal gossip, legal comment, I instantly and precociously perceived a case of entail-by-custom, dragging on perhaps for years, a very pretty thing for Mr. Pascoe. It might well ruin the farm, did the Sylvesters contest; it would be a very pretty thing for a local man. . . .

What dismayed me far more than even this possibility was the revelation of such new treachery as no Sylvester yet dreamed of. Fanny and Charles designed to sell the land.—This thought formulated, I found my tongue.

"But Charlie won't sell!" I cried. "He won't want to! I think *you'd* better tell Mr. Pascoe *that!*"

Miss Jones laughed again.

"And I believed you in Fanny's confidence!" said she. "Why, it was all agreed between them upon their very engagement!—But never mind, my dear; we shall all meet yet at their Plymouth villa. Do I see my horrid chariot approach? Add, when you write, I shall expect in future a dog-cart at least!"

Mr. Granville the butcher halted at her gesticulations; and took her up, and they drove off towards Frampton. I went back into the house, to my Aunt Grace, and said baldly,

"Aunt Grace, suppose Fanny makes Charles sell the farm?"

It was like asking, suppose the skies fall? My question made no more, and no less impression. My Aunt Grace took me by the shoulders, turned my face to the window, and called to Rachel to put hot bricks in my bed. "'Tis but a chill 'ee've taken," said my Aunt Grace reassuringly. "Twelve hours' sleep, and 'ee'll be brave as ever!" I reiterated a desperate, probably incoherent warning. "Us have allowed 'ee to fret beyond measure," said Rachel anxiously. "Bide still, my lamb, till I bring 'ee a cup of hot milk. . . ." Between warmed sheets, fed hot milk, and bread and honey, I couldn't but take a little comfort before I slept; but slept only to wake again, long before midnight struck.

3

SUCH wakings belong to childhood: because their character is universal—the strangeness of a room unlit, all other rooms of a house still bright, the sense of adult life still active, even the world without still about its business—I lay a moment or two back in London, where I waked so not uncommonly. Dim window-shape, dim shapes of furniture, told me where I was; recollection rushed in upon me and I remembered danger, and my Aunt Charlotte absent; and myself of all Sylvester kin the only one on guard. . . .

From no sensible motive, I slipped from my bed to the window. I had forgotten—half-asleep—that it no longer looked out upon the crab-tree court. Only small nondescript roofings met my eye, between which no doppelgänger started. But it was again a very hot, still night. The wood of the window-seat again warmed my knees, as the wood of the sill warmed my elbows. I was in the attitude for prayer; I prayed.

I prayed no prayer that had been taught me. Church twice-on-Sunday furnished no suitable form. We had prayers, at

school, each morning, rather beautifully spoken by our head-
mistress, from which I personally derived an emotion rather
aesthetic than religious. I now petitioned my Maker crudely
as a missionary's first convert, baldly as an Archbishop in time
of war. I prayed help *us*, defeat them; and in return I will be
good.

Then I went back to bed; and the next day Charlotte came
home.

CHAPTER XXIII

I

WHAT passed in London, during those five days, I learned, essentially, from two sources: Clara Blow and my father. My Aunt Charlotte wasn't uncommunicative by intent: she was simply incapable of detailed, coherent narrating, all we were to learn from Charlotte came out piecemeal, over a period, literally, of years. Moreover she couldn't possibly, because she had no idea of it, give us any proper account of her own personal impact upon Jackson's Economical Saloon.

I wish I had seen my Aunt Charlotte in London. She must have cut through our streets like a ship in full sail. Even Clara Blow's vocabulary could scarcely do her justice—as Clara was first to admit. "Chrissake!" said Clara—repeatedly. "If you'd been there when she sailed in! I mean, Charlie we'd sort of got used to, after all he's a man, but when your Auntie sailed in, dear, my word, didn't Jackson's look small!"

I prefer to go back a little further: to the descent of Fanny and my Aunt Charlotte upon the Flower in Hand. Here Charlotte, with her Norfolk connections, was immediately recognized as a guest not to be trifled with; and one very old waiter, who remembered her father, was more or less detailed to her service. My Aunt Charlotte looked him over, put a searching question or two, and handed over the egg-basket. All other fare, said she, they'd eat cold; but he might make them tea as required, the caddy to be returned at their departure. (She left the last half-dozen eggs as a vail, also the heel of a pasty.) I imagine Fanny impressed at once by this display of authority. I imagine her no less impressed, for all her Plymouth sophistication, when Charlotte, their baggage deposited and their subsistence assured, commanded a cab to bear them to Brocket Place.

This was on the day of their arrival; they reached Jackson's Economical Saloon at a rather good moment—tables set, all culinary preparations under way, the evening mob not yet in evidence. I suppose Jackson's looked as well as ever it could; and Clara Blow had just done her hair.

You could have knocked her down with a feather; chiefly, she subsequently assured me, from the shock of recognition. "'Cause I recognized her, naturally, straight off," said Clara Blow. "I mean, there can't be many of 'em, can there? I mean, that *size!* I'm fairly whopping myself," said Clara Blow, "but I give you my word, dear, when your Auntie sailed in, I felt no bigger than a cat.—There was two little fellows eating saveloys, and Chrissake, *they* looked like mice."

So my Aunt Charlotte's introduction of herself was superfluous—and of Fanny Davis scarcely less so. Clara took a dislike to Fanny at once. Addressing Charlotte, she said *she* was Miss Blow; and if Mrs. Sylvester wanted Charlie, he'd be down in two shakes. (There was never any mention, in all Clara's highly detailed narrative, of her having given Charlie a shout. I presumed her not unwilling to see him knocked down by a feather too.) Charlotte and Fanny then accepted seats, and what immediately ensued was a contest in hospitality, country versus town.

My Aunt Charlotte had in a basket cheese, cold chicken and fruit-cake. Clara Blow had Jackson's. As Charlotte pressed chicken on Clara, Clara pressed sausage-rolls on Charlotte. It was a form of courtesy understood and appreciated by both, and smoothed over any slight awkwardness; indeed, food being to both a natural preoccupation, and with so many varieties of it at hand, they rapidly fell into a very enjoyable exchange. It became technical: Clara Blow detailed Jackson's catering-system, with a side-glance at the bandit-like practices of London tradespeople, and Charlotte told how Sylvesters, but for salt and sugar, could live fatly off their own land. They interested each other; they stimulated each other. Ideas began to form—the idea, for example, of Jackson's serving chicken on Sundays, the fowls to be sent direct from Devon, thus cutting out the middle-man. "I do believe it might catch on," said Clara Blow, concentrating. "Let alone raising the tone, I do believe it might pay. I've a good mind to speak to Mr. Isaacs. . . ."

I can well imagine how irritating this was to Fanny Davis. Too ladylike to eat, strung to a high pitch of emotional tension, she had to sit and listen to the best ways of packing poultry. Also, she was being ignored. I feel certain that my Aunt Charlotte was quite unsubtle in this, that she talked catering to Clara because catering interested her, not to irritate Fanny Davis; but the effect on Fanny must have been irritating nonetheless. As for Clara—"Here, let's hear what *you* say!" shouted she to the saveloy-eaters. "How'd you fancy a proper Sunday dinner—chicken and all trimmings, ninepence a plate?"—and when they doubtfully shook their heads, found time, even as

Charlie's foot shook the stair, to shout back, "All right, then, a tanner; with bread."

Then Charlie came in.

2

You could have knocked him down with a feather. He admitted it himself, when Clara asked him afterwards. At the moment, however, he simply stood. They all stood, even the genuine customers, who rather hastily paid and left. ("As though they expected something to *happen*, dear," reported Clara Blow. "Though what I'm sure I can't say. There was nothing like a row.")

What did happen was that Charlotte walked up to her son, and took a good, close look at him, and kissed him, as she did so rarely, only when he left home or returned to it, once on the cheek. Neither of them spoke; but their bearing made on Clara at least a very strong impression. She said she half-expected to see them turn about and walk off together, as though there was no one else in the Saloon. And so I too think they might have done—but for Fanny Davis.

At last seizing her cue, Fanny flung herself forward upon Charlie's neck, and hung there like a bat, and burst into a flood of happy tears. Clara Blow instantly plucked her away and dropped her back upon a chair. There, Fanny's happy tears turned to hysteria. Clara, no doubt swearing like a trooper, dashed a glassful of water over her, then from an ingrained habit of cleaning up rubbed her dry with a napkin. When all this was over Charlie and my Aunt Charlotte still hadn't stirred.

"Charlie bor," said my Aunt Charlotte moderately, "it seems 'ee be a bone of contention."

She had to speak rather loudly, to top Fanny's sobs; but as she turned enquiringly to Clara, these rapidly diminished.

Fanny Davis too turned to Clara Blow; who was fortunately able to repeat to me her very words. I didn't wonder she remembered them, for they were notable.

"Mrs. Sylvester, I wouldn't take him as a gift," said Clara Blow. "I am a person never wanted bread yet, nor ever will. I make no claim upon him whatsoever; if he has accepted of my hospitality, he's earned, with a bit of pushing, his keep. Far be it from me to offend a lady I both esteem and admire, and I hope we may still have a mutual business connection in the future; but I wouldn't take Charlie as a gift."

So spoke, or said she spoke, Clara Blow. (Doubtless she polished it up a bit afterwards. I have equally no doubt that she gave me a generally accurate outline.)

"That be plain talk at least," said my Aunt Charlotte approvingly, "and seems the field be left clear for Fanny Davis. (Who'm miraculously recovered," threw in Charlotte superfluously.) "Well, Charlie bor?"

What Charles would have answered was never known, Fanny Davis being now in full voice again.

"Field left clear, indeed!" cried she. "*Oh,* what hypocrites am I fallen among! Are not Charles and I engaged? Haven't we been engaged these two years? Haven't we but waited till I regained strength, to marry? Charles, my love, tell your mother the truth! Admit your debts, which we have come to pay! Let Miss Blow list every last item—since for all her fine talk don't we know how she holds you? For heaven's sake, my love, speak!"

I don't know if Clara generously polished up this speech too, I can say only that it sounds exactly like Fanny Davis. And I think Charles really must have spoken at last. Almost incredibly, my Cousin Charles hadn't yet uttered a single word; but I think he must have spoken then—only Taffy Griffiths saved him.

3

"WHICH was really a riot, dear," said Clara Blow. "Not that I refer to any roughness—far from it! I mean just the way your Auntie handled matters. Six-to-seven-to-eight, Jackson's commonly quiet as a graveyard, chaps never as a rule turning up much before nine; only it just so happened—as it *would* so happen—Taffy Griffiths brought some friends in for a sausage-and-mash before the fight. I think it was the Welterweight. And being mostly Welsh, dear, they do incline to sing a bit; which I must say, their voices being almost professional, I've always looked on it as rather an attraction. It was the *words*, dear," said Clara frankly, "upset your Auntie. So she told them to clear out."

"Did they?" asked I, enthralled.

"That's the funny part," said Clara Blow. "They did. Without Charlie raising a finger, what's more. Of course they saw him *ready*, but really he wasn't needed. Your Auntie just gave 'em a proper tongue-lashing, and out they skedaddled—five bob lost to the till, but I still say well worth it . . ."

And when Taffy Griffiths and his friends had vanished, so had my Cousin Charles. With them, in fact. Under cover of the riot, mingling with Taffy's friends, my Cousin Charles simply walked out.

"Clara!" I protested. "Oh, Clara, how *could* he?"

"Well, dear, he never did like an upset," said Clara tolerantly. "That's what made him such a splendid chucker-out."

So my Cousin Charles walked quietly out; and the three women left behind, their bone of contention no less than the arbiter of their fates withdrawn, faced something of an anti-climax. (The shepherd Paris on Mount Ida might equally have discountenanced three goddesses.) Fanny Davis was probably quite right to grow hysterical again, she could have done nothing more socially useful. By common consent the whole debate was postponed; and Clara Blow went out and found another cab, and in it my Aunt Charlotte and Fanny Davis returned to the Flower in Hand.

I have omitted the fact that they there shared a room. Economy, prudence, convention—every possible consideration made it inevitable. But I have often wondered what sort of a night they spent, side by side in the same double bed.

CHAPTER XXIV

I

My Aunt Charlotte at least slept sufficiently well to have energy, next day, for quite extensive sight-seeing.

She visited the Tower of London, Madame Tussaud's Waxworks, St. Paul's Cathedral and Westminster Abbey; and if such a programme in the circumstances smacks of frivolity, I can but repeat her subsequent explanation to my Aunts Grace and Rachel: she had never visited London before, and in all probability never would again. My Aunts Grace and Rachel accepted this unhesitatingly, and only marvelled how Charlotte got about. (She got about in omnibuses. She found their conductors very civil. She found the police very civil also. In fact, my Aunt Charlotte found all London very civil to her. I see the trail of staggered Cockneys in her wake. She was such a great, good-humoured, handsome Whopper.) Moreover, she had already complete faith in Clara Blow's ability to produce Charlie when and as required; and so after a substantial breakfast off her own eggs and bacon set out to see the sights.

Fanny Davis, on the other hand, relapsing into fragility, took breakfast in bed, and didn't set off on her own account until considerably later. Thus their paths for the major part of Wednesday diverged; and in any case I very much doubt whether Charlotte would have followed Fanny Davis'. My Aunt Charlotte's big nature included several delicacies: I was domiciled at the farm summer after summer, but she never felt this gave her a claim to my parents' London hospitality, because I was paid for at some infinitesimal sum per week. Fanny Davis' object, that Wednesday, was to visit my father and cadge free legal advice.

2

OF this episode I heard far more than I wished as soon as I got home.

"If you have ever insinuated," said my father, "to any of your mother's down-at-heel Devonshire connections, that I am open to a little pettifogging rural business—such as might arise, for example, over a parcel of disputed hen-coops, or some bucolic breach-of-promise—I shall be greatly obliged if you will disillusion them."

It was then I knew Fanny Davis had visited him. He couldn't possibly so refer to my Aunt Charlotte—and how strongly I wished it had been she, not Fanny, who bearded him! I felt even my father must have recognized Charlotte's quality. I was too much afraid of him to point out that Fanny Davis wasn't a Sylvester at all. I simply stammered I was sorry, I hadn't insinuated anything . . .

My father had nonetheless been subjected to persecution. I felt at the time, as I feel now, his language exaggerated. Fanny Davis merely caught him at lunch. By a piece of luck, she found him lunching at home. (He in fact quite often came home to lunch while my mother was away, to enjoy the emptiness of the house. There could have been no other reason, since all our cooks thought he did it to keep them up to the mark, and in revenge served specially unappetising food.) Nor did Fanny actually interrupt his repast; our experienced parlourmaid Toptree kept her waiting in the hall till he had finished, and announced her only with the coffee. (This again an act of revenge: one glance must have identified Fanny Davis, to any experienced eye, as a person one wasn't at home to. Toptree hadn't quite the audacity to interrupt the master's lunch, so compromised on annoying him at his coffee. Parlourmaids also resent being kept up to the mark.) To my father at his coffee, and at his first cigar of the day, Fanny Davis therefore entered; and instantly made on him the worst possible impression.

"I admit," said my father, with elaborate irony, "to a certain astonishment. Some moon-calf charged with poaching, even with manslaughter: some collapsed hayrick of a rustic matron, anxious for her young at the Assizes: either well-worn character, however hopelessly beyond my aid, would have surprised me less. Indeed, would have offended me less. A milliner involved in breach-of-promise I found offensive absolutely . . ."

How did he guess Fanny Davis a milliner? I didn't like to ask. And as I didn't think she'd *told*, I could only imagine Fanny Davis' millinerishness undisguisable as ineradicable. Leaving the point aside, I nervously enquired what my father had said.

"I instructed her, naturally, to go away," said he, "and take advice of some local man."

So my father and Miss Jones agreed. Miss Jones also was a

milliner; I didn't think my father would be quite pleased to know of this second opinion, so to speak, so thoroughly in agreement with his own. At the time—for this particular conversation took place in the autumn, all the events of the summer behind me—I was chiefly concerned to re-establish Sylvester repute. It wasn't easy. Toptree, who listened throughout at the dining-room door, reported Fanny Davis' recital of her wrongs enough to blacken every Sylvester living. ("Crimes you usually find only in the Bible," said Toptree, with relish. "Only to think, miss, of a young lady among such folk! I wonder your Ma don't shudder.") My father undoubtedly took much the same view. (Allying himself, however unconsciously, now with a parlourmaid. No one ever pointed this sort of thing out to him, which was a pity. His opinion of himself, because never challenged, in time led him to such impatience with the slightest opposition that we couldn't even have people to dinner.) Fortunately my mother proved more broad-minded: she hadn't encountered Fanny Davis personally, and my own healthy looks afforded so good an excuse for not taking me to Bournemouth with the boys, she would never hear an anti-Sylvester word. *All* county families, said she, had their hangers-on: my father had acted with exactly his usual good judgment in warning off one of the Sylvesters': so there was no reason in the world for my ceasing to frequent them. "I don't suppose the child knows a thing about it—whatever the imbroglio may be," said my mother; in which opinion, as may be imagined, I loyally backed her. In time, the row subsided.

The fact relevant to Fanny Davis' and my Aunt Charlotte's London expedition was that Fanny failed to enlist my father's aid.

She thus wasted the major part of Wednesday altogether. (Charlotte at least saw the sights.) They rejoined forces, if such a term may stand, late that afternoon: when Charlotte coming in to rest her feet found Fanny once more prone upon the double bed. After a short breathing-space Charlotte again ordered a cab capable of penetrating to Brocket Place.

"Though if 'ee don't wish to accompany I," said she considerately, "I'll bear Charlie your kind regards."

Of course Fanny Davis accompanied her.

3

MY Cousin Charles was upstairs, sleeping it off.

Clara Blow told Charlotte this at once. Where he'd been, night before, she couldn't say, except with Taffy Griffiths—and undoubtedly up to no good, because he hadn't come back till after noon. "And then sick as a dog, dear," said Clara Blow, with less than her usual tolerance. "I don't say he can't *take* it, Mrs. Sylvester, no more'n I'd say a man ain't 'titled, time to time, to his skinful. Only Charlie I must say *can* take it . . ." "Devon cider be a powerful brew," said my Aunt Charlotte, perhaps a touch complacently. "London gin's a sight worse," retorted Clara, suddenly sharp. "Which Charlie ought to be got off. I must say this is the first time I've ever seen signs on him; and I must say I don't like it."

From a person who wouldn't take Charlie as a gift, this was disinterested. Charlotte looked at her kindly; and after remarking there was plenty of time to let he slumber an hour or two more, tactfully asked to see the kitchen. Clara flounced ahead,

with some difficulty my Aunt Charlotte was manoeuvred down
a ladder-like stair into Jackson's subterranean base of operations.
(What she saw there was never described. But recalling subsequent, reiterated exclamations of thankfulness that they'd
borne their own provision, I suspect every horror save cockroaches. I don't think there could have been cockroaches, because the exterminator was in that Spring.) Fanny Davis, who
refused to accompany them, remained seated above in the
Saloon.

There they left her, and there she stayed. She didn't take
the bolder step of going up to Charlie. Delicacy forbade. Victoria was on the throne, and Fanny Davis nothing if not re-
fined. She was greatly ambitious, and quite ruthless, she would
have sold up the Sylvester farm, thrust, ruthlessly, all Sylvesters into whatever almshouse could accommodate them:
delicacy nonetheless forbade her to risk encountering Charlie
unbreeched. So she sat and waited; and doubtless fretted, and
felt angry as I did at my Aunt Charlotte's lavish attitude to
time. Fanny Davis, to be sure, fretted only an hour or so,
whereas I, two summers before, fretted months; but hers was
the more painful suspense.

When Clara and my Aunt Charlotte returned, they made a
light supper. After what Charlotte must have seen below, I
find her appetite for sausage-rolls, (as reported to me by Clara),
little short of heroic. Heroic in courtesy, she ate five. Clara,
equally courteous, but more easily, ate Charlotte's cold chicken;
and Fanny Davis ate nothing. If all ears pricked equally at any
sound from above—and Clara told me she once quite jumped,
but it was only Charlie falling off the bed—at least Clara and
Charlotte had chat to cover their preoccupation.—Quite possibly

my Aunt Charlotte wasn't preoccupied at all; she never could think of two things at once, she knew Charlie safe to hand upstairs, and the notion of supplying Jackson's with poultry was one to appeal to her most strongly. She had an excellent business-sense, unfortunately frustrated by her epoch; she could have run the farm, but for her sex, as well as any Sylvester male. The possibility of purveying Jackson's opened as it were a door; to-day I see her supplying half London's hotels . . .

So the hour, the hours passed insensibly: a scattering of early customers called Clara to duty, my Aunt Charlotte noted thoughtfully what each one ate, and what each one paid. The money thrown about astonished her—a penny for a saveloy, a halfpenny for pease-pudding; all mounting up to shillings. (I may say that she kept an eye on Jackson's thenceforward. My Aunt Charlotte was a pioneer of the country-to-London cater-ing trade.) Nor was she in the least put out by the raffish aspect of most of Jackson's customers. She *expected* raffishness, in London; and since even the ungodly had to eat, why shouldn't the righteous profit? Moreover—and this sentiment, uttered some months later, I particularly cherish—why shouldn't even the ungodly, if they paid, purchase wholesome food? "Did our Lord, when Him so miraculously multiplied loaves and fishes," enquired Charlotte pertinently, "enquire which mouths be-longed to church-goers? Wherefore no boiling-fowl goes forth as a roaster, even into the jaws of London chaps . . ."

I glance too far ahead. We are still in Jackson's Economical Saloon, Wednesday evening, waiting for Charlie to sleep it off.

He appeared about nine o'clock: washed, dressed, in the pink of condition, and obviously prepared with some arrange-ment of words. He had something in his mind to utter; and surveying the three women ranged before him, but with an eye seeking Clara Blow, immediately spoke.

"Do Taffy Griffiths look in ere midnight," said my Cousin Charles, "him'll require hot food for eight."

To both Clara Blow and my Aunt Charlotte these words were absolutely welcome. Each felt towards Charles identically. Each in her way desired nothing so much as to see him accept responsibility. He was now doing so, as regarded Jackson's Economical Saloon; and though but upon a trifle, his words, after the long winter of his indifference, were like snowdrops, presaging a better season. Clara Blow's swift rejoinder, up till one-two-three kitchen's ready for 'em, was a blackbird's shout. . . .

Then it was—upon this springtide, and possibly to find Charlie's London spring-tide run against her—that my Aunt Charlotte spoke out.

"Charlie bor," said she, "to see 'ee completely master of all business here be most peculiarly gratifying. And do 'ee choose to bide in London, where Miss Blow reports 'ee already so looked up to, no word of mine shall call 'ee home. But do 'ee aim to return, I'll not deny 'twill rejoice all hearts; seeing the farm also in sad need of management. And do 'ee return wedded to Fanny Davis, again no word shall be spoke. All us asks be, how do 'ee decide?"

She took a risk, and she must have known it, in putting the alternative so squarely to him. It would have been so easy for my Cousin Charles, that easy-going male, to loll a little longer on Clara Blow's, and Jackson's, ample bosom. He took by nature the line of least resistance. My Aunt Charlotte put it to him squarely—with a rider.

"Though this I must state also," said she, "that do 'ee choose to remain from home, I b'aint able to promise 'ee any 'countable inheritance. Your father Tobias ain't able, bor; and what's masterless land but common? So why not wed wi' Fanny Davis, and return?"

I cannot imagine, even now, how she guessed Fanny Davis keeping him *away*. Obviously her whole gamble was based on the assumption; but to every other view Fanny was drawing him back. Charlotte couldn't tell herself; she simply guessed it. And having guessed, how bold was her approach! She wanted Charles home, without Fanny; backed her guess, and by opening her arms to both, forced Charles at last to frankness, and the point.—That Fanny Davis was instantly on his neck probably rather helped than hindered.

"Yes, Charles, *yes!*" cried Fanny wildly. "*Oh*, what a relief, what a blessing, to find your mother take our part! Hasn't it been but my weakness kept you from me?—Now what shall prevent our marriage, and your return?"

So at last Charlie spoke to the point. He had to. He saw his mother pressing on his marriage to Fanny Davis, with what consequences he alone knew; he saw Clara determined to cast him off for ever; his nostrils smelled Devon soil, he saw the weeds over-grow his own rightful Sylvester land. So he spoke. He said baldly,

"I be more anxious to return than words can tell. Two years since I saw my Dad not able. I be more anxious to return than all the world. But not do it mean wedding Fanny."

The ensuing confusion of sound must have been immense. "Charles, Charles, my love!" shrieked Fanny Davis. "Chrissake, what the hell's he at now?" shouted Clara Blow. "Bor, think what 'ee say!" adjured my Aunt Charlotte. "Why shouldn't 'ee wed the poor toad?"

I imagine the straggle of early patrons—for this whole interesting scene was not unwitnessed: Clara Blow, from her trade, and all Sylvesters by nature, had an aristocratic indifference to publicity—I imagine Jackson's few early patrons awaiting Charlie's reply almost as eagerly as his interlocutors.

"*Ask* she," said my Cousin Charles, "what Plymouth-town have to offer a chap like I."

So broke upon my Aunt Charlotte what I already knew: Fanny Davis' intent to see the farm abandoned. Fanny instantly, naturally denied it; my Cousin Charles, with equal stubbornness, persisted in full confession. He wanted to get all out and done with; and as late as the following summer was still relieving his mind to myself.

4

" 'Twas all *her* doing," said my Cousin Charles, "as I don't now mind telling 'ee. . . ."

When I heard my Cousin Charles' tale, it surprised me even more than had Fanny's. For love at first sight, for the *coup de foudre,* how many novelettes had not prepared me? Not one of them had prepared me for Charles' peculiarly unromantic rôle of hero in spite of himself.

As a lover, he was modest, opportunist, easy-going and unconvinced.

He never attempted to deny making love to Fanny Davis. What astounded me was to hear him say he thought 'twould be respectful. *"Respectful?"* I repeated incredulously. "Seeing she bound to my Uncle Stephen," explained Charles. "I thought to pleasure 'em both by my attentions. . . ." He was one of the stupidest men, my Cousin Charles, I have ever met. But he was also honest. "I'll not deny," he admitted, "that Fanny in her fine blue gown made it easy to I. I'd seen no such fashionable females in Australia. And her have a trick of looking beneath her eyelids, 'ee can call naught but enticing . . . Her enticed I," said my Cousin Charles frankly.

"But you must," I persisted, "you must have *said* something to her, at the Assembly? Something, I mean, to make her give up Uncle Stephen?"

He looked vague.

"Maybe," he agreed, vaguely. "Home cider be a powerful brew, and us filled ourselves proper ere setting out. Maybe I did swear a bit more undyingness than suited."

If I had been the size of my Aunt Charlotte, I would have shaken him.

"But didn't you see, next day, what you'd done? Didn't you see Fanny would wait for you?"

He smiled.—The sweet Sylvester smile, so rare, so disproportionately effective, changed his whole face. I, angry as I was, melted before it.

"B'aint that true?" said my Cousin Charles thoughtfully. "They wait . . ." (How many in Australia alone, thought I?) "But where Fanny had the pull, do 'ee see, was that *her* was to home . . . Guarding my interests. 'Twas so her put it in her letters: guarding my interests. So naturally I was bound to reply, to keep she still."

"By Miss Jones," said I, "because you were ashamed to write direct!"

He considered; finally, with the eternal Sylvester motion, shook his big, handsome head.

"Fanny was right enough there," said he. "Letters, save at proper tides, be too astounding for folk's comfort; moreover the sight of my first might well have brought all to light.— But the damned time I spent penning 'em! 'Twas hard labour, no less," said Charles earnestly, "and specially as Clara couldn't aid I."

"And why," I asked severely, "not?"

"Stands to reason," said my Cousin Charles. "One female b'aint penning to another love and de-vo-ti-on, on behalf of the same chap."

He was incorrigible. I understand him now better than I did then—but still with the reservation: incorrigible. Yet his handsomeness wasn't his fault; nature had made him so handsome he couldn't walk down a street without attracting every female glance. He was as handsome as his father Tobias, and as mild as his Uncle Stephen. The one Sylvester quality he lacked was will. Looking back, I am astounded that no one had married him sooner. He escaped, I imagine, as the jelly-fish escapes the shore-fisher's net; by sheer amorphousness . . .

But he had in full measure the cardinal Sylvester quality of all. He had the Sylvester feeling for land.

"Did Fanny ever tell 'ee," he asked me once, "of her design I should sell up the farm? Us to bide in Plymouth, so landless as rats? But for that, I'd maybe have returned and out-faced all; I never did see Stephen a match for she . . ."

So Fanny Davis, with all her boldness, and all her resolution, defeated her own ends. She saw her chance and seized it, she enticed Charles Sylvester, eldest son of eldest son, and during those first days of her illness, while he so kindly relieved the women-watchers, bound him firmly with a promise to wed. Then she over-reached herself.—"For I took it," said Charles, "as naught but a passing fancy, due to her mysterious disease; hearing she speak so pretty and wistful of Plymouth, I took it as but passing weakness. So to cheer she, I agreed."

This was so like Charles, I instantly believed him. And I knew how beguiling Fanny could be, weak and helpless on bed or sofa, cooing out soft complaint in her wooing, beguiling voice . . . But when her letters began to arrive in London, each more pressing than the last—urging him, for example, to visit my father and get expert opinion on his rights—then my Cousin Charles took alarm. He saw Fanny so determined on her outrageous plan, he was literally afraid to come home.

"For I feared her'd get hold of I again," said Charles frankly, "or at the very least, did I hold out, create some most 'mazing disturbance. So I saw naught for it, but to bide at London."

So he bided in London two years. The original plan, as concocted by Fanny Davis, was that he should stay there perhaps a couple of months, seeing and taking opinion of my father while Fanny prepared the ground at the farm. Charles stayed a couple of years, more or less easily reposed upon the bosom of Clara Blow.—He had all the Sylvesters' lavish attitude to time; no doubt he'd have stayed ten years, or twenty, peaceably chucking-out Jackson's clientèle, sooner than face any 'mazing disturbance at home. . . .

"You should have married Clara straight away," said I.

He looked at me with genuine reprobation.

THE GIPSY IN THE PARLOUR

"And I betrothed to Fanny Davis?" said my Cousin Charles. He was incorrigible.

5

AGAIN I have leapt forward in time. My Aunt Charlotte, and my Cousin Charles, and my friend Clara Blow, and Fanny Davis, are still in Jackson's Economical Saloon, embattled.

CHAPTER XXV

I

FANNY fought hard. She employed every resource of pathos, guile and venom. When Charlie's complete, and completely unchivalrous defence left her in the end no leg to stand on, at least as regarded the farm, and when her counterattack, that she'd thought only of his welfare, was almost contemptuously turned aside by Charlotte, Fanny abandoned this position altogether to retreat upon the higher ground of true love. Her affections so thoroughly belonged to Charles, even after his heartless treatment of her, she was prepared to live out her days a simple farmer's wife. Gladly, at her beloved's side, would she work her fingers to the bone, seeking no reward but his and his family's good opinion. My Cousin Charles, with one eye on Clara, who ostentatiously began to count saveloys, replied uncomfortably but firmly, he was sorry, but all that was over. "Is it possible!" cried Fanny Davis piteously. "Oh how is it possible you should say so!" My Cousin Charles said he didn't 'xactly know; but so 'twas, and he was very sorry. (On this ground he didn't defend himself at all. He let Fanny, as her temper rose, call him every name she could think of, and when she dissolved back into tears, obligingly allowed her to hang on his neck again.) On the ground of true love Fanny had

233

it all her own way—in fact my Aunt Charlotte, temporarily
changing sides, helped her give Charles a thorough dressing-
down. Clara Blow also contributed several cutting observations
on men of weak character. At this phase of the battle it was
undoubtedly Charles who took most punishment; but his
wounds couldn't help Fanny to victory. If he wouldn't marry
her, he wouldn't. His head was bloody but unbowed.

Fanny Davis accordingly changed front once more; wiped
her eyes, sweetened her voice, forgave my Cousin Charles absolutely, and observed what a fortunate thing it was dear Stephen hadn't been *told*.

The implications of this magnanimity were lost on no one.
Clara Blow told me afterwards she could hardly believe her
ears: she knowing enough already of how all lived, at the farm,
to foresee the extraordinary discomfort, particularly to Charlie's
future wife, of having Fanny Davis permanently on the prem-
ises. Which was of course exactly what Fanny foresaw herself,
as with a sweet, forgiving smile she went on to assure my
Cousin Charles that never, never, never, by word or look, would
she remind him of what had once passed between them.

"For indeed, dear Mrs. Toby," said she, turning her honey
now upon Charlotte, "I have learned my lesson. Hardly taught,
to be sure, by lips I believed loving to me! I *have* been ambitious, I acknowledge it—though only for Charles. I *have* allowed my heart to sway me, against my promised word. But
no more ambition, no more foolhardy loving, shall ever again
turn me from the strict path of duty to dear Stephen."

I have always thought Clara Blow remarkably generous in
her reporting of Fanny's speeches. She never played them
down, if anything she polished them up. (She was a great

patron of melodrama.) This one, said Clara, would have touched a heart of stone.

Fortunately my Aunt Charlotte's partook more of the nature of oak.

"What my brother Stephen be ignorant of as yet," said she stolidly, "him shall learn upon the instant us returns. That is, do 'ee return with I, Fanny Davis; and for all his kind, forgiving nature, knowing what him shall, and against the word of all his kindred, him'll not take 'ee to wife, Fanny Davis. Howsoever—" the oak being the noblest of trees, and my Aunt Charlotte carved from its heartwood—"howsoever," continued she, "I do acknowledge, and with Miss Blow a most sensible and experienced person to witness, certain lightness on my son Charlie's part in his dealings wi' 'ee. Therefore, morning-time, us may make rounds of a milliner or two, I having noted more than one announcement on my travels, seeking experienced bonnet-hands. And do a matter of five-ten pounds be needed, to give 'ee proper standing or partnership, that Sylvesters shall furnish. Now b'aint it getting late?"

This unexpected conclusion, rhetorically perhaps weak, in effect couldn't have been bettered, because it *was*. Even for Jackson's, it was getting late. Tables were filling, Taffy Griffiths was due, and the life of the Saloon, like the life of the farm, carried on across all human hazards. Charlotte, who had been listened to by both Charlie and Clara Blow with extreme admiration, by these last words returned them to their proper business. Clara started towards the kitchen, my Cousin Charles flexed his shoulders; and this sudden switch took the wind from Fanny's sails. It was as though the strong vitality of the Sylvesters, of Clara Blow, even of the Saloon itself, once again and for the last time elbowed her aside.

"Speak out your mind if 'ee wish, though there be none to hear," said my Aunt Charlotte comfortably. "In my opinion, 'ee'd do better to revolve what all must consider very fair words; which, in my opinion again, 'ee can do best in bed. Can 'ee endure to pass another night with I, Fanny Davis?"

Fanny snapped. Caught in a trap of her own making, she snapped.

"Certainly!" said she. "Just so Sylvesters can foot the bill, certainly!—if you're not afraid I'll stuff *poison* down your throat!"

"Did I think 'ee had means of procuring it, maybe I'd not take the chance," said Charlotte placidly. "Moreover, I hear London police-chaps be uncommon sharp. Charlie bor, fetch we a cab."

So that night too they slept side by side.

2

My Aunt Charlotte devoted the whole of Thursday to Fanny Davis.

She was no longer worried about Charles. She knew where he was, and why, and perceived his return home now simply a matter of paying his railway-fare: Fanny she had still on her hands, a Sylvester responsibility. A lesser woman might have felt all responsibility cancelled by Fanny's behaviour; my Aunt Charlotte worked it out in her mind, and could subsequently give Grace and Rachel excellent reasons for every act. Stephen

undeniably bore Fanny from Plymouth, her native place—
where presumably she would have behaved better, and Charlie
undeniably turned her head at the Assembly, and made she
promises he'd no business to, and by raising her ambitions
paved the way to all following wickedness: wherefore Sylvesters, though naturally anxious, and entitled, to rid themselves of she, had still the duty to Fanny Davis of seeing her
decently placed.

The pair of them therefore spent Thursday going round
bonnet-shops.

Fanny Davis went because there was nothing else she could
do. She had no money, and even her return-ticket was in
Charlotte's pocket. She had lost, and at some point during the
night must have faced the fact. But she went unwillingly. Charlotte was astonished: to her mind the prospect of living in
London should have been Fanny's best cure—so sophisticated
as she was, with such a taste for urban life. In shop after shop,
however, Fanny seemed determined to make the worst possible
impression. When asked what experience she had, she replied,
Only in the country. ("Plymouth be by some considered a town
of size," suggested Charlotte. "Not as regards fashion," said
Fanny Davis loudly. "As regards fashion, it's a *wilderness*.")
When asked if she were strong, she instantly said no, she was
subject to fainting-fits; and in fact felt worse for London air.
Only when asked what wages she would take were her standards metropolitan; and then so outrageously so, every prospec-
tive employer at once showed her the door.

The truth of course was that London had rebuffed Fanny
Davis too thoroughly. She had been rebuffed at Jackson's, and
rebuffed by my father. Even the streets rebuffed her; after her

two-years' seclusion in our parlour she understandably found their noise and bustle terrifying. (She never summoned Charlotte's courage to see the sights. Except for her one foray to my home, and her cab-journeys to Jackson's, she spent her every London-moment in a double bedroom at the Flower in Hand.) And when at the end of Thursday's reconnoitring she cast all sophistication aside, and whimpered that if she were left in London she would die, my Aunt Charlotte, considering her peaked white face, was reluctantly forced to admit it possible.

When my Aunt Charlotte thought of Plymouth, it seemed a better plan still—so obviously, she wondered she hadn't pitched on it sooner. For wasn't Plymouth Fanny's home? (Charlotte, I believe, to the end of her days blamed Fanny's uprooting for all that followed. She was extraordinarily cautious, at the farm, of transplanting so much as a bush. She said all plants throve best where they rooted.) Wasn't Plymouth Fanny's home—filled with old friends, old associations? Wouldn't all old acquaintance there remember her, and cry, "Look, here's Fanny Davis back"?

These very considerations made Fanny prefer death in London. She had quitted Plymouth in some glory: cocked aloft, both physically and socially, upon a bridegroom's pony-cart; off to her wedding, bound for the desirable state of matrimony. One or two spinster-cronies, yellow with envy, actually threw old shoes . . . To return amongst them still spinster-named was more than flesh and blood, said Fanny Davis, could possibly endure; and hinted at making away with herself altogether in preference.

My Aunt Charlotte, munching pastry in the Flower in

Hand's best bedroom, (Fanny too nervous to eat downstairs), after due consideration admitted this natural enough.

So it was they came round to Frampton; where Miss Jones, said Fanny Davis, had long sought genteel assistance; and whose privity to Fanny's sad past, by offering the relief of confidence, would make Fanny's present sad lot less totally unendurable. . .

3

I STILL find it almost incredible that this was in fact the solution.

Fanny Davis returned with Charlotte as far as Frampton, and was there set down to join forces with her friend Miss Jones. Some five-ten pounds was I believe put up for her, buying her into this most modest partnership, and in Frampton Fanny Davis, through all the years of my adolescence, fabricated bonnets for local swells.—Even for the Sylvesters. Her tongue never for a day left them alone, and the Sylvesters cared so little, my aunts regularly bought their bonnets from her. ("*Charlotte, what's she to do here?*" "*Trim up our bonnets,*" *said Charlotte, laughing.*) After my Cousin Charles married, his wife bought bonnets. I myself occasionally bought a chip straw hat. An extraordinary indifference to opinion, an unawareness of anything not directly touching *land*, carried my Sylvester connections through, or over, all. . . .

My Uncle Stephen's passage must have been the most painful; but he was so nearly a saint, he traversed it. We had to tell him. My Aunt Charlotte, I am sure with the greatest sympathy and feeling, told him—if not all, at least enough to make him resign himself. Fanny Davis was indeed recovered; but not sufficiently so to contemplate matrimony; and so preferred to return to her old avocation. "Her requiring," explained my Aunt Charlotte, "some little bustle of business to keep up her spirits; which in our quiet life, how can us hope to furnish?" My Uncle Stephen, Sylvester-like, nodded a big, resigned head. He didn't seem very much put out. Bachelorhood was become second nature to him, and he never had thought himself worthy of Fanny Davis.—To her my Aunt Charlotte spoke less smoothly. "Though 'ee mayn't think Sylvesters able for much," said she, "us can still run 'ee out of Frampton, do us care to tell a tale or two." "Of Charles' jilting me?" rejoined Fanny coolly. "Can't *I* tell a tale of *him?*" "Ah, but 'ee be on the losing end of it," said my Aunt Charlotte. "Live and let live, Fanny Davis; and before all things keep your wiles from my brother Stephen, for I'll not see he fooled twice. Why not have a try for Mr. Pascoe?" suggested my Aunt Charlotte. "'Ee be no worse-looking than Miss Jones?"

So Fanny Davis left my Uncle Stephen alone, while continuing to loose her venom on the Sylvesters. This proved extremely good for trade. In so quiet a neighbourhood any fresh local feud was always welcome as a source of entertainment, and if no one ever got to this one's exact root, no one the less enjoyed Fanny's shafts, so that it became rather a popular thing to buy bonnets off her, to hear what she'd say next.—Of this whole tale, I sometimes see this the most remarkable chapter. Fanny Davis, set up with Miss Jones as Frampton's fashionable milliner, to the end of her life enjoyed all Sylvester custom. Her tongue was never still, she abused, in

casual conversation, to each least, casual customer, every one of
my aunts. The stream of libel issuing from her shop supplied
the scandal-pool of Frampton. My aunts never ceased to buy
their bonnets from her. They said she made them fit properly
to the back of the head. They cared no more for what Fanny
said of them than for the braying of a gipsy's donkey, strayed
back into the Sylvester court.

4

I RETURN again to London. My Aunt Charlotte is not yet
home.

She could really have come back on Friday. The several
small matters to be settled with Clara Blow might have been
attended to on Thursday evening, by cabbing round to the
Saloon as usual. (My Aunt Charlotte's insouciant use of this
phrase was a wonder and a joy.) That she didn't, and that she
chose to spend a whole day more in London, was due solely
to the fact that she was enjoying herself. Unlike Fanny Davis,
she found London purely delightful—not that she'd care to
bide there, she reassured us, but as a most wonderful, interesting
sight to which even three-four days barely did justice. Her
strong nerves, her strong self-confidence, carried her easily
through all noise and bustle; she found Londoners, as has been
said, most 'mazingly civil, and their shops proper master-
pieces. Her own anxieties relieved, the thought that we at
home might be anxious still never crossed her mind. (As regards all except myself she was of course right.) So she took
Friday morning as a holiday, to look at the shops.

THE GIPSY IN THE PARLOUR

This morning Fanny Davis did not accompany her. She was too fatigued to stir, even at Charlotte's reminder that it was probably their first-and-last chance. Charlotte set out for Regent Street leaving Fanny Davis still in bed. ("I trust 'ee don't aim to play the same game twice," said Charlotte. "If 'ee can't accompany I to the train tomorrow morning, Fanny Davis, in London 'ee'll have to bide." Fanny murmured, for once sincerely, all she needed was a single day's rest.) Charlotte therefore set out alone, passed a most enjoyable morning, returned to the Flower in Hand for the only food she trusted, and there, to set the crown on her pleasure, and make her feel a proper Londoner indeed, found a note from Clara Blow.

Clara invited her specially to Jackson's that afternoon, because it was then Mr. Isaacs came in for his weekly review of the takings. Clara thought Mrs. Sylvester and Mr. Isaacs ought to meet. The urchin who bore this missive still lurked about the entry; Charlotte rewarded him with a slice of fruit-cake, and cabbed round to Jackson's as usual.

The gist of what passed between her and Mr. Isaacs was of course known to all of us later; Clara Blow's own, more general report was that they got together straight off. They got together on chickens, and pigs; my Aunt Charlotte at once expanding Clara's original thought of chicken-dinners, (which both she and Mr. Isaacs saw as idealistic), to embrace such more workaday viands as sausages, trotters, and Bath chaps. Whatever she said, Mr. Isaacs listened to. ("Him 'course not half her size," related Clara Blow, "and your Auntie, I don't know if you've ever noticed it, kind of naturally behaving like as if wherever she is belongs to her.") For whatever reason, my Aunt Charlotte rapidly established over Mr. Isaacs such an empire, he readily agreed to accept, in London, whatever comestibles she could dispatch to him; which commercial treaty happily agreed, Charlotte retired to the kitchen with Clara Blow, took two-three minutes to settle two-three small matters of business with *her,* and cabbed it, (as usual), back to the Flower in Hand.

Her parting remark to Clara was that she'd had a very nice time.

Back at the Flower in Hand, she found Fanny Davis still prostrate. A whole last evening in London offered possibilities only to Charlotte. We never knew, we never knew for certain; but we think she went to a Music Hall.

CHAPTER XXVI

I

THUS when on the Saturday my Aunt Charlotte returned, she bore none but good news. Fanny Davis, shed on the way, at Frampton, at Miss Jones', was already paying her entertainment in scandal. What mattered it to us, at the farm? We had Charlotte's heartening tale to hear, we had the parlour to show Charlotte, I recall my Aunt Rachel and myself playing 'Chopsticks' so late as seven o'clock. Even my uncles appeared pleased, by Charlotte's return: and she had all arguments out at once, publicly, over the supper-table, the moment she reassumed her place there. "Tobias," said she, "your son Charlie have made the greatest fool of he alive, but what's past's to be let go by." She paused; Tobias didn't speak. His side of the argument was conducted as usual in silence.—And indeed hardly existed: Charlotte, thoroughly back to her old form, rejuvenated by her London exploits, was in fettle to tame all my uncles put together, and in their prime, and the old man to boot, just as she'd tamed them thirty years earlier. "Howsoever," continued Charlotte, "him being protected by what us may only call the natural Sylvester thick-headedness, all may yet turn for the best; so I'll just tell 'ee now all 'ee needs to know. Firstly, 'ee owes Stephen twenty pound. Secondly, Fanny Davis bides at

Frampton, trimming bonnets wi' Miss Jones. Third and lastly, Charlie's to wed, and such a wife as him scarce deserves. Now let one of 'ee great images speak grace."

It was my Uncle Stephen who rose. Charlotte had had her private word with him earlier, and his long, sad face was already set in lines of resignation and composure.—He alone of the Sylvester men had at that moment a distinct personality: he looked already the lay-preacher he was soon to become.

"Oh Lord, if 'Ee've been trying we somewhat, past year or two," prayed my Uncle Stephen—at once pitching on a tone of such intimacy, the rest of us were a little disconcerted— "mayn't 'Ee take Charlotte's London journey into consideration? Which her undertook for naught save Fanny's good?" (Though our heads were all properly bowed, I caught a glance between Grace and Rachel which possibly referred to Charlotte, cabs and shops. However, we could all pray along our own lines.) "Wherefore, Oh Lord," continued my Uncle Stephen, "seeing us have done all in our power for one so specially afflicted by Thee—since without doubt 'twas Thy will even London doctoring but half succeeded; and seeing my brother's son Charlie about to return home at last, with us do hope a most suitable female, Thy blessing, Oh Lord, be most particularly requested; also upon this food."

Then we all fell to.

2

In the heat of a blazing September noon, in a parlour brilliant at every point—lustre-ware shining in the cabinet, andirons bright about the hearth—the three famous Sylvester women waited to receive and make welcome the fourth.

Themselves matched the day. Layered chin to toe in flannel, cambric, and silk at a guinea a yard, their broad cheeks crimson, their temples beaded with sweat, my aunts stood big and florid and jocund as three big suns. I, on this occasion rather prominent, hovered at the parlour's threshold; so, looking back, observed and enjoyed the splendid sight. My Aunt Charlotte stood a pace in advance, but my Aunts Grace and Rachel flanked her closely. From time to time they exchanged some probably ribald jest—by me scarcely caught, not at all understood, nonetheless heightening the general mood of strong hilarity. There was naturally no male Sylvester present, they were all afield. My uncles saw no reason in the world to come in, from harvesting, to greet someone they would see daily for the rest of their lives.

Charlie entered first—but only by an instant. Clara bounded immediately upon his heels. She bounded straight past him into my Aunt Charlotte's embrace—just dealing me, *en passant*, a loving wallop. The tumult broke out, indeed, before Charles himself got fairly in; he must have known at once he'd brought home another Sylvester woman.

"Chrissake!" shouted Clara Blow. "Chrissake, ain't it all lovely?"—and my Aunt Charlotte immediately boxed her ears.

3

So one saw at once it was going to be all right. Because in the first place Clara wasn't knocked down, which spoke volumes

247

for her solid weight, and in the second, she wasn't affronted. She was startled, for a moment; glanced sideways at me, instantly perceived that I wasn't the cause for so explicit a rebuke, and apologised.

"I've got into a coarse way of talking," said Clara Blow frankly. "Don't hold it against me, just bash me when I forget. I'll be grateful."

"To speak so, I see 'ee'll make me a very good daughter indeed," returned Charlotte placidly. "In such a place as Jackson's, where no doubt all example was against 'ee, 'ee might be excused; but in my house never utter such blasphemous words again, Clara Blow—and in the meantime, let I show 'ee your chamber."

They streamed out, the four big women, on such an impetus of energy and good-will that Charlie backed before them from the door. I might have followed. Clara was my friend, in a sense my discovery, I might have run officiously before to open doors, point out beauties, listen to her (censored) cries of admiration. But I didn't. I stayed in the parlour by myself. The big, glowing room persuaded me: the clock persuaded me, whose tick, after so long a silence, seemed to beat more strongly than ever. It was like the renewed, steady heart-beat of the house. There was plenty of time. I promised myself long, leisurely explorations with Clara Blow, when I had her undivided attention. The little busybody in me already astir again, I determined to take particular pains with her language. In the meantime, I stayed in the parlour.

What I now best remember is the sunlight: refracted from brass about the hearth, prisms over the mantel, the glass of the lustre-ware cabinet. It was the sunniest room, my aunts' parlour, I have ever known. I, idly tinkling out 'Bluebells,' sat with the sun on the nape of my neck. It was so warm, I have never felt sun so warm since.

I felt more deeply happy than ever since. It all happened, this whole story, a long time ago.

72
74
75
76
77
79
83
85